IF YOU CAN'T STAND THE HEAT...

JOSS WOOD

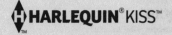

Recycling programs
for this product may
not exist in your area.

ISBN-13: 978-0-373-20729-9

IF YOU CAN'T STAND THE HEAT...

www.Harlequin.com

ABOUT JOSS WOOD

—

Joss Wood wrote her first book at the age of eight and has never really stopped. Her passion for putting letters on a blank screen is matched only by her love of books and traveling—especially to the wild places of Southern Africa—and possibly by her hatred of ironing and making school lunches.

Fueled by coffee, when she's not writing or being a hands-on mum, Joss, with her background in business and marketing, works for a nonprofit organization to promote the local economic development and collective business interests of the area where she resides. Happily and chaotically surrounded by books, family and friends, she lives in KwaZulu-Natal, South Africa, with her husband, children and their many pets.

Other Harlequin® KISS™ titles by Joss Wood:

It Was Only a Kiss

This and other titles by Joss Wood are available in ebook format—check out **Harlequin.com.**

For their love and support, I have so many friends to thank. Old friends, new friends, coffee friends and crying friends. Friends who know me inside out and friends I've just met. But, because we share a friendship based on raucous laughter, craziness, sarcasm, loyalty and love, this book is especially dedicated to Tracy, Linda and Kerry.

IF YOU CAN'T STAND THE HEAT...

ONE

_____

'ELLIE, YOUR PHONE _is ringing! Ellie, answer it now!'_

Ellie Evans grinned at her best friend Merri's voice emanating from her mobile in her personalised ring tone, then eagerly scooped up the phone and slapped it against her ear.

'El?'

'Hey, you—how's the Princess?' Ellie asked, sorting through the invoices on her desk, which essentially meant that she just moved them from one pile to another.

'The Princess' was her goddaughter, Molly Blue, a six-month-old diva who had them all wrapped around her chubby pinkie finger. Merri launched into a far too descriptive monologue about teething and nappies, interrupted sleep and baby food. Ellie—who was still having a hard time reconciling her party-lovin', heel-kickin', free-spirited friend with motherhood—_mmm_-ed in all the right places and tuned out.

'Okay, I get the hint. I'm boring,' Merri stated, yanking

Ellie's attention back. 'But you normally make an effort to at least pretend to listen. So what's up?'

Her friend since they were teenagers, Merri knew her inside out. And as she was her employee as well as her best friend she had to tell her the earth-shattering news. Sitting in her tiny office on the second floor of her bakery and delicatessen, Ellie bit her lip and stared at her messy desk. Panic, bitter and insistent, crept up her throat.

She pulled in a deep breath. 'The Khans have sold the building.'

'Which building?'

'This building, Merri. We have six months before we have to move out.'

Ellie heard Merri's swift intake of breath.

'But why would they sell?' she wailed.

'They are in their seventies, and I would guess they're tired of the hassle. They probably got a fortune for the property. We all know that it's the best retail space for miles.'

'Just because it sits on the corner of the two main roads into town and is directly opposite the most famous beach in False Bay it doesn't mean it's the best...'

'That's exactly what it means.'

Ellie looked out of the sash window to the beach and the lazy ocean beyond it. It had been a day since she'd been slapped with the news and she no longer had butterflies about Pari's, the bakery that had been in her family for over forty years. They had all been eaten by the bats on some psycho-drug currently swarming in her stomach.

'Why can't we just rent from the new owners?'

'I asked. They are going to do major renovations to

attract corporate shops and intend on hiking the rents accordingly. We couldn't afford it. And, more scarily, Lucy—'

'The estate agent?'

'Mmm. Well, she told me that retail space is at a premium in St James, and there are "few, if any" properties suitable for a bakery-slash-coffee-shop-slash-delicatessen for sale or to rent.'

After four decades of being a St James and False Bay institution Pari's future was uncertain, and as the partner-in-residence Ellie had to deal with this life-changing situation.

She had no idea what they—she—was going to do.

'Have you told your mum?' Merri asked quietly.

'I can't get hold of her. She hasn't made contact for ten days. I think she's booked into an ashram...or sunning herself in Goa,' Ellie replied, her voice weary. Where she *wasn't* was in the bakery, with her partner/daughter, helping her sort out the mess they were in.

Your idea, Ellie reminded herself. *You said she could go. You suggested that she take the year off, have some fun, follow her dream...* What *had* she been thinking? In all honesty it had been a mostly symbolic offer; nobody had been more shocked—horrified!—than her when Ashnee had immediately run off to pack her bags and book her air ticket. She'd never thought Ashnee would leave the bakery, leave *her*...

'El, I know that this isn't a good time, especially in light of what you've just told me, but I can't put it off any longer. I need to ask you a huge favour.'

Ellie frowned when she picked up the serious note in Merri's voice.

'Anything, provided that you are still coming back to work on Monday,' Ellie quipped. Merri was a phenomenal baker and Ellie had desperately missed her talent in the bakery while she took her maternity leave.

The silence following her statement slapped her around the head. Oh, no...no, no, *no*! 'Merri, I need you,' she pleaded.

'My baby needs me too, El.' Merri sounded miserable. 'And I'm not ready to come back to work just yet. I will be, but not just yet. Maybe in another month. She's so little and I need to be with her...please? Tell me you understand, Ellie.'

I understand that I haven't filled your position because I was holding it open for you—because you asked me to. I understand that I'm running myself ragged, that the clients miss you...

'Another month?' Merri coaxed. 'Pretty please?'

Ellie rubbed her forehead. What could she say? Merri didn't need to work, thanks to her very generous father, so if she forced her to choose between the bakery and Molly Blue the bakery would lose. *She* would lose...

Ellie swallowed, told herself that if she pushed Merri to come back and she didn't then it was her decision... but she felt the flames of panic lick her throat. They were big girls, and their friendship was more than the job they shared—it would survive her leaving the bakery—but she didn't want to take the chance. Her head knew that she was overreacting but her heart didn't care.

She had too much at stake as it was. She couldn't risk

losing her in any way. She'd coped for over six months; she'd manage another month. Somehow.

Ellie bit her top lip. 'Sure, Merri.'

'You're the best—but I've got to dash. The Princess is bellowing.' Now Ellie could hear Molly's insistent wail. 'I'll try to get to the bakery later this week and we can talk about what we're going to do. Byeee! Love you.'

'Love you...' Ellie heard the beep-beep that told her the call had been dropped and tossed her mobile on the desk in front of her.

'El, there's someone to see you out front.'

Ellie glanced from the merry face of Samantha, one of her servers, peeking around her door to the old-fashioned clock above her head, and frowned. The bakery and coffee shop had closed ten minutes ago, so who could it be?

'Who is it?'

Samantha shrugged. 'Dunno. He just said to tell you that your father sent him. He's alone out front...we're all heading home.'

'Thanks, Sammy.' Ellie frowned and swivelled around to look at the screens on the desk behind her. There were cameras in the front of the shop, in the bakery and in the storeroom, and they fed live footage into the monitors.

Ellie's brows rose as she spotted him, standing off to the side of a long display of glass-fronted fridges, a rucksack hanging off his very broad shoulders. Week-long stubble covered his jaw and his auburn hair was tousled from finger raking.

Jack Chapman. Okay, she was officially surprised. Any woman who watched any one of the premier news channels would recognise that strong face under the shaggy hair. Ellie wasn't sure whether he was more famous for his superlative and insightful war reporting or for being the definition of eye candy.

Grubby low-slung jeans and even grubbier boots. A dark untucked T-shirt. He ran a hand through his hair and, seeing a clasp undone on the side pocket of his rucksack, bent down to fix it. Ellie watched the long muscles bunching under his thin shirt, the curve of a very nice butt, the strength of his brown neck.

Oh, *yum*—oh, stop it now! Get a grip! The important questions were: why was he here, what did he want and what on earth was her father thinking?

Ellie lifted her head as Samantha tapped on the doorframe again and stood there, shuffling on her feet and biting her lip. She recognised that look. 'What's up, Sammy?'

Samantha looked at her with big brown eyes. 'I know that I promised to work for you tomorrow night to help with the *petits fours* for that fashion show—'

'But?'

'But I've been offered a ticket to see Linkin Park and they are my favourite band...it's a free ticket and you know how much I love them.'

Ellie considered giving her a lecture on responsibility and keeping your word, on how promises shouldn't be broken, but the kid was nineteen and it *was* Linkin Park. She remembered being that age and the thrill of a kick-ass concert.

And Samantha, battling to put herself through university, couldn't afford to pay for a ticket herself. She'd remember it for for ever...so what if it meant that Ellie had to work a couple of hours longer? It wasn't as if she had a life or anything.

'Okay, I'll let you off the hook.' Ellie winced at Samantha's high-pitched squeal. 'This time. Now, get out of here.'

Ellie grinned as she heard her whooping down the stairs, but the grin faded when she glanced at the monitor again. Scowling, she reached for her mobile, hastily scrolling through her address book before pushing the green button.

'Ellie—hello.' Her father's deep voice crooned across the miles.

'Dad, why is Jack Chapman in my bakery?'

Ellie heard her father's sharp intake of breath. 'He's there already? Good. I was worried.'

Of course you were, Ellie silently agreed. For the past ten years, since her eighteenth birthday, she'd listened to her father rumble on and on about Jack Chapman—the son he'd always wanted and never got. 'He's the poster-boy for a new generation of war correspondents,' he'd said. 'Unbiased, tough. Willing to dive into a story without thinking about his safety, looking for the story behind the story, yet able to push aside emotion to look for the truth...' Yada, yada, yada...

'So, again, why is he here?' Ellie asked.

And, by the way, why do you only call when you want something from me? Oh, wait, you didn't call. I did! You just sent your boy along, expecting me to accommodate your every whim.

Some things never changed.

'He was doing an interview with a Somalian warlord

who flipped. He was stripped of his cash and credit cards, delivered at gunpoint to a United Nations aid plane leaving for Cape Town and bundled onto it,' Mitchell Evans said in a clipped voice. 'I need you to give him a bed.'

Jeez, Dad, do I have a B&B sign tattooed on my forehead?

Ellie, desperate to move beyond her default habit of trying to please her father, tried to say no, but a totally different set of words came out of her mouth. 'For how long?'

God, she was such a wimp.

'Well, here's the thing, sugar-pie...'

Oh, good grief. Her father had a *thing*. A lifetime with her father had taught her that a thing *never* worked out in her favour. 'Jack is helping me write a book on the intimate lives of war reporters—mine included.'

Interesting—but she had no idea what any of this had to do with *her*. But Mitchell didn't like being interrupted, so Ellie waited for him to finish.

'He needs to talk to my family members. I thought he could stay a little while, talk to you about life with me...'

Sorry...life with him? What life with him? During her parents' on-off marriage their home had been a place for her mum to do his laundry rather than to live. He'd lived his life in all the countries people were trying to get out of: Iraq, Gaza, Bosnia. Home was a place he'd dropped in and out of. Work had always been his passion, his muse, his lifelong love affair.

Resentment nibbled at the wall of her stomach. Depending on what story had been consuming him at the time, Mitchell had missed every single important event of her childhood. Christmas concerts and ballet recitals, swimming galas and father-daughter days. How could he be expected to be involved in his daughter's life when there were bigger issues in the world to write about, analyse, study?

What he'd never realised was that he was her biggest issue...the creator of her angst, the source of her abandonment issues, the spring that fed the fountain of her self-doubt.

Ellie winced at her melodramatic thoughts. Her childhood with Mitchell had been fraught with drama but it was over. However, in situations like these, old resentments bubbled up and over.

Her father had been yakking on for a while and Ellie refocused on what he was saying.

'The editors and I want Jack to include his story—he *is* the brightest of today's bunch—but getting Jack to talk about himself is like trying to find water in the Gobi Desert. He's not interested. He's as much an enigma to me as he was when we first met. So will you talk to him?' Mitchell asked. 'About me?'

Oh, good grief. Did she have to? Really?

'Maybe.' Which they both knew meant that she would. 'But, Dad, seriously? You can't just dump your waifs and strays on me.' He could—of course he could. He was Mitchell Evans and she was a push-over.

'Waif and stray? Jack is anything but!'

Ellie rubbed her temple. Could this day throw anything else at her head? The bottom line was that another of Mitchell's colleagues was on her doorstep and she could either take him in or turn him away. Which she wouldn't do...because then her father wouldn't be pleased and he'd sulk, and in twenty years' time he'd remind her that she'd let him down. Really, it was just easier to give the guy a bed for the night and bask in Mitchell's approval for twenty seconds. If that.

If only they were *normal* people, Ellie thought. The last colleague of her father's she'd had to stay—again at Mitchell's request—had got hammered on her wine and tried to paw her before passing out on her Persian carpet. And every cameraman, producer and correspondent she'd ever met—including her father—was crazy, weird, strange or odd. She figured that it was a necessary requirement if you wanted to chase down and report on human conflicts and disasters.

Mitchell's voice, now that he'd got his own way, sounded jaunty again. 'Jack's a good man. He's probably not slept for days, hasn't eaten properly for more than a week. A bed, a meal, a bath. It's not that much to ask because you're a good person, my sweet, sweet girl.'

My sweet, sweet girl? Tuh!

Sweet, sweet sucker, more like.

Ellie sneaked another look at Mr-Hot-Enough-to-Melt-Heavy-Metal. He did have a body to die for, she thought.

'Have you met Jack before?' Mitchell asked.

'Briefly. At your wedding to Steph.' Wife number three, who'd stuck around for six months. Ellie had been eighteen, chronically shy, and Jack had barely noticed her.

'Oh, yeah—Steph. I liked her...I still don't know why she left,' Mitchell said, sounding plausibly bemused.

Gee, Dad, here's a clue. Maybe, like me, she hated the idea of the man she adored being away for five of those six months, plunging into the situation in Afghanistan and only popping up occasionally on TV. Hated not knowing whether you were alive or dead. It's no picnic loving someone who doesn't love you a fraction as much as you love your job.

She, her mother and Mitchell's two subsequent wives had come second-best time after time...decade after decade. And she'd repeated the whole stupid cycle by getting engaged to Darryl.

She'd vowed she'd never fall in love with a journalist and she hadn't. But life had bust a gut laughing when she'd become engaged to a man she'd thought was the exact opposite of her father, only to realise that he spent even less time at home than her father had. That was quite an accomplishment, since he'd never, as far as she knew, left London itself.

She'd been such a sucker, Ellie thought. Still was...

Maybe one of these days she'd find her spine.

Ellie looked down at her mobile, realised that her father hadn't said goodbye before disconnecting and shrugged. Situation normal. She glanced at the monitor again and saw the impatience on Jack's face, caught his tapping foot. The muscles in his arms bulged as he folded them across his chest. Although the feed was in black and white she knew that his eyes were hazel...sometimes brown, sometimes green, gold, always compelling. Right now they were blazing with a combination of frustration, exhaustion and a very healthy dose of annoyance.

He was different from the twenty-four-year-old she'd met a decade ago. Older, harder, a bit damaged. Ellie felt an unfamiliar buzz in her womb and cocked her head as attraction skittered through her veins and caused her heartbeat to fuzz...

She tossed her mobile onto her desk and pushed her chair back as she stood up and blew out a breath.

It didn't matter that he was tall, built and had a sexy face that could stop traffic, she lectured herself. Crazy came in all packages.

'Jack?'

Jack Chapman, standing in the front section of the bakery—aqua stripes on the walls, black checked floors, white cabinets, a sunshine-yellow surfboard—whirled around at the low, melodious voice and blinked. Then blinked again. He knew he was tired, but this was ridiculous...

He'd been expecting the awkward, overweight, shy girl from Mitch's wedding not this...*babe*! This tropical, colourful, radiant, riveting, dazzling babe. With a capital B. In bold and italics.

Waist-length black hair streaked with purple and green stripes, milk-saturated coffee skin, vivid blue eyes and her father's pugnacious chin.

And slim, curvy legs that went up to her ears.

'Hi, I'm Ellie. Mitchell has asked me to put you up for the night.'

His pulse kicked up as he struggled to find his words. He eventually managed to spit a couple out. 'I'm grateful. Thank you.'

Whoa! Jack dropped his pack to the floor and resisted the impulse to put his hand on his heart to check if it was okay. With his history...

You are not *having a heart attack, you moron! Major over-reaction here, dude, cool your jets!*

So she wasn't who he'd been expecting? In his line of work little was as expected, so why was his heart jumping and his mouth dry?

Jack rocked on his heels, looked around and tried not to act like a gauche teenager. 'This is a really nice place. Do you own it?'

Ellie looked around and the corners of her mouth tipped up. 'Yep. My mum and I are partners.'

'Ah...' He looked at the empty display fridges. 'Where's the food? Shouldn't there be food?'

Her smile was a fist to his sternum.

'Most of the baked goods are sold out and we put the deli meats away every night.' She fiddled with the strap of her huge leather tote bag. 'So, how was your flight?' she asked politely.

Sitting on the floor of a cargo plane in turbulence, with bruised ribs and a pounding headache? Just peachy. 'Fine, thanks.'

The reality was that he was exhausted, achingly stiff and sore, and his side felt as if he had a red-hot poker lodged inside it. He wanted a shower and to sleep for a week. His glance slid to a fridge filled with soft drinks. And he'd kill someone for a Coke.

Ellie caught his look and waved to the fridge. 'Help yourself.'

Jack grimaced. 'I can't pay for it.'

'Pari's can afford to give you a can on the house,' Ellie said wryly.

The words were barely out of her mouth and he was opening the fridge, yanking out a red can and popping the tab. The tart, sugary liquid slid down his throat and he sighed, knowing the sugar and caffeine would give him another hour or two of energy. Maybe...

He swore under his breath as once again he realised that he was stuck halfway across the world. He couldn't even pay for a damn soft drink. He silently cursed again. He needed to borrow cash and a bed from Ellie until his replacement bank cards were delivered. He grimaced at the sour taste now in his mouth. Having to ask for help made him feel...out of control, helpless. Powerless.

He hated to feel beholden, but he reminded himself it would only be for a night—two, maximum.

Jack finished his drink and looked around for a bin.

Ellie took the can from him, walked behind the counter and tossed it away. 'Help yourself to another, if you like.'

'I'm okay. Thanks.'

Ellie's eyebrows lifted and their eyes caught and held. Jack thought that she was an amazing combination of east and west: skin from her Goan-born grandparents, and blue eyes and that chin from her Irish father. Her body was all her own and should come with a 'Danger' warning. Long legs, tiny waist, incredible breasts...

Because he was very, very good at reading body language, he saw wariness in her face, a lot of shyness and a hint of resignation. Could he blame her? He was a stranger, about to move into her house.

'Funky décor,' he said, trying to put her at ease. Hanging off the wall next to the front door was a fire-red canoe; its seating area sprouting gushing bunches of multi-coloured daisy-like flowers. 'I don't think I've

ever seen surfboards and canoes used to decorate before.
Or filled with flowers.'

Ellie laughed. 'I know; they are completely over the
top, but such fun!'

'Those daisy things look real,' Jack commented.

'Gerbera daisies—and I don't think there's a point to
flower arrangements if they aren't real,' Ellie replied.

He'd never thought about flowers that way. Actually,
he'd never thought about flowers at all. 'What's with the
signatures on the canoe?'

Ellie shrugged. 'I have no idea. I bought it like that.'

Jack shoved his hand into the pocket of his jeans and
winced when the taxi driver leaned on his horn. Dammit, he'd forgotten about *him*. He felt humiliation tighten
his throat. Now came the hard part, he thought, cursing
under his breath. A soft drink was one thing...

'Look, I'm really sorry, but I've got myself into a bit of
a sticky situation... Is there any chance you could pay the
taxi fare for me? I'm good for it, I promise.'

'Sure.' Ellie reached into her bag, pulled out her purse
and handed him a couple of bills.

Jack felt the tips of his fingers brush hers and winced
at the familiar flame that licked its way up his arm. His
body had decided that it was seriously attracted to her
and there was nothing he could do about it.

Damn, Jack thought, as he stomped out through the
door to pay his taxi fare. He really didn't feel comfortable
being attracted to a woman he was beholden to, who was
his mentor's beloved daughter and with whom he'd spend
only two days before blowing out of her life.

Just ignore it, Jack told himself. *You're a grown man, firmly in control of your libido.*

He blew air into his cheeks as he handed the money over to the taxi driver and rubbed his hand over his face. The door behind him opened and he turned away from the road to see Ellie lugging his heavy rucksack through the door. Ignoring his burning side, he broke into a jog, quickly reached her and took his pack from her. The gangster bastards had taken his iPad, his satellite and mobile phones, his cash and credit cards, but had left him his dirty, disgusting clothes.

He would've left them too...

'Here—let me take that.' Jack took his rucksack from her.

'I just need to lock up and we can go,' Ellie said, before disappearing back inside the building.

Jack waited in the late-afternoon sun on the corner, his rucksack resting against an aqua pot planted with hot-pink flowers. He was beginning to suspect—from her multi-coloured hair and her bright bakery with its pink and purple exterior—that Ellie liked colour. Lots of it.

Mitchell had mentioned that Ellie was a baker and he'd expected her to be frumpy and housewifey, rotund and rosy—not slim, sexy and arty. Even her jewellery was creative: multi-length strands of beads in different shades of blue. He could say something about lucky beads to be against that chest, but decided that even the thought was pathetic...

He heard the door open behind him and she reappeared. She pulled the wooden and glass door shut, then yanked down the security grate and bolted and locked it.

Jack looked from the old-style bakery to the wide beach across the road and felt a smile form. It was nearly half-past six, a warm evening in summer, and the beach and boardwalk hummed with people.

'What time does the sun set?' he asked.

'Late. Eight-thirty-ish,' Ellie answered. She gestured to the road behind them. 'I live so close to work that I don't drive...um...my house is up that hill.'

Jack looked up the steep road to the mountain behind it and sighed. That was all he needed—a hike up a hill with a heavy pack. What else was this day going to throw at him?

He sighed again. 'Lead on.'

Ellie pulled a pair of over-large sunglasses from her bag and put them on, and they started to walk. They passed an antique store, a bookstore and an old-fashioned-looking pharmacy—he needed to stock up on some supplies there, but that would raise some awkward questions. He waited for Ellie to initiate the conversation. She did, moments later, good manners overcoming her increasingly obvious shyness.

'So, what happened to you?'

'Didn't your father tell you?'

'Only that you got jumped by a couple of thugs and were kicked out of Somalia. You need a place to stay because you're broke.'

'Temporarily broke,' Jack corrected her. Mitchell hadn't given her the whole story, thankfully. It was simple enough. He'd asked a question about the hijackings of passing ships which had pushed the warlord's 'detonate' button. He'd gone psycho and ordered his henchman to beat the crap out of him. He'd tried to resist, but six against one...bad odds.

Very bad odds. Jack shook off a shudder.

'So, is there anything else I can do for you apart from giving you a bed?'

Her question jerked him back to the present and his instinctive answer was, *A night with you in bed would be great.*

Seriously? *That* was what he was thinking?

Jack shook his head and ordered himself to get with the programme. 'Um...I just need to spend a night, maybe two. Borrow a mobile phone, a computer to send some e-mails, have an address to have my replacement bank cards delivered to...' Jack replied.

'I have a spare mobile, and you can use my old laptop. I'll write my address down for you. Are you on a deadline?'

'Not too bad. This is a print story for a political magazine.'

Ellie lifted her eyebrows. 'I thought you only did TV work?'

'I get the occasional assignment from newspapers and magazines. I freelance, so I write articles in between reporting for the news channels,' Jack replied.

Ellie shoved her sunglasses up into her hair and rubbed her eyes. 'So how are you going to write these articles? I presume your notes were taken.'

'I backed up my notes and documents onto a flash drive just before the interview. I slipped it into my shoe.' It was one of the many precautionary measures he took when operating in Third World countries.

'They let you keep your passport?'

Jack shrugged. 'They wanted me to leave and not having a passport would have hindered that.'

Ellie shook her head. 'You have a crazy job.'

He did, and he loved it. Jack shrugged. 'I operate best in a war zone, under pressure.' He loved having a rucksack on his back, dodging bullets and bombs to get the stories few other journalists found.

'Mitchell always said that it's a powerful experience to be holed up in a hotel in Mogadishu or Sarajevo with no water, electricity or food, playing poker with local contacts to the background music of bombs and automatic gunfire. I never understood that.'

Jack frowned at the note of bitterness in her voice and, quickly realising that there was a subtext beneath her words that he didn't understand, chose his next words carefully. 'Most people would consider it their worst nightmare—and to the people living and working in that war zone it is—but it *is* exciting, and documenting history is important.'

And the possibility of imminent death didn't frighten him at all. After all, he'd faced death before...

No, what would kill him would be being into a nine-to-five job, living in one city, doing the same thing day in and day out. He'd cheated death and received a second swipe at life...and the promise he'd made so long ago, to live life hard and fast and big, still fuelled him on a daily basis.

Jack felt a hard knot in his throat and tried to swallow it down. He was alive because someone else hadn't received the same second swipe...

'We're here.'

Ellie's statement interrupted his spiralling thoughts

and Jack hid his sigh of relief as she turned up a drive-way and approached a wrought-iron gate. Thank God. He wasn't sure if he could go much further.

Ellie looked at the remote in her hand, took a breath and briefly closed her eyes. He saw the tension in her shoulders and the rigid muscle in her jaw. She wasn't comfortable... Jack cursed. If he had been operating on more than twelve hours' sleep in four days he would have picked up that the shyness was actually tension a lot ear-lier. And it had increased the closer they came to her home.

'Look, you're obviously not happy about having me here,' Jack said, dropping his pack to the ground. 'Sorry. I didn't realise. I'll head back to the bakery—hitch a lift to the airport.'

Ellie jammed her hands into the pockets of her cut-offs. 'No—really, Jack...I told my father I'd help you.'

'I don't need your charity,' Jack said, pushing the words out between his clenched teeth.

'It's not charity.' Ellie lifted up a hand and rubbed her eyes with her thumb and index finger. 'It's just been a long day and I'm tired.'

That wasn't it. She was strung tighter than a guitar string. His voice softened. 'Ellie, I don't want you to feel uncomfortable in your own home. I told Mitch that I was happy to wait at the airport. It's not a big deal.'

Ellie straightened and looked him in the eye. 'I'm sorry. I'm the one who is making this difficult. Your arrival just pulled up some old memories. The last time I took in one of my father's workmates I was chased around my house by a drunken, horny cameraman.'

He sent her his I'm-a-good-guy grin. 'Typical. Those damn cameramen—you can't send them anywhere.'

Ellie smiled, as he'd intended her to. He could see some of her tension dissolve at his stab at humour.

'Sorry, I know I sound ridiculous. And I'm not crazy about talking about my relationship with Mitchell for this book you're helping him write—'

'I'm *helping* him write? Is that what he said?' Jack shook his head. Mitchell was living in Never-Never Land. It was *his* book, and *he* was writing the damn thing. Yes, Mitchell Evans's and Ken Baines's names would be on the cover, but there would be no doubt about who was the author. The sizeable advance in his bank account was a freaking big clue.

'Your father...I like him...but, jeez, he can be a pain in the ass,' Jack said.

'So does that mean you don't want to talk to me about him?' Ellie asked, sounding hopeful and a great deal less nervous.

Jack half smiled as he shook his head. 'Sorry...I do need to talk to you about him.'

He raked his hair off his face, thinking about the book. Ken's fascinating story was all but finished; Mitch's was progressing. Thank God he'd resisted all the collective pressure to get him to write his. Frankly, it would be like having his chest cracked open without anaesthetic.

He was such a hypocrite. He had no problems digging around other people's psyches but was more than happy to leave his own alone.

Jack looked at Ellie, saw her still uncertain expression

and was reminded that she was wary of having a strange man in her house. He couldn't blame her.

'And as for chasing you around your house? Apart from the fact that I am so whipped I couldn't make a move on a corpse, it really isn't my style.'

Ellie looked at him for a long moment and then her smile blossomed. It was the nicest punch to the heart he'd ever received.

TWO

———

JACK LOOKED UP a lavender-lined driveway to the house beyond it. It was a modest two-storey with Old World charm, wooden bay windows and a deep veranda, nestled in a wild garden surrounded by a high brick wall. The driveway led up to a two-door garage. He didn't do charming houses—hell, he didn't do *houses*. He had a flat that he barely saw, boxes that were still unpacked, a fridge that was never stocked. In many ways his flat was just another hotel room: as impersonal, as bland. He wasn't attached to any of his material possessions and he liked it that way.

Attachment was not an emotion he felt he needed to become better acquainted with...either to possessions or partners.

'Nice place,' Jack said as he walked up the stairs onto a covered veranda. Ellie took a set of keys from the back pocket of those tight shorts. It *was* nice—not for him, but nice—a charming house with loads of character.

'The house was my grandmother's. I inherited it from her.'

Jack glanced idly over his shoulder and his breath caught in his throat. *God, what a view!*

'Oh, that is just amazing,' he said, curling his fingers around the wooden beam that supported the veranda's roof. Looking out over the houses below, he could see a sweeping stretch of endless beach that showed the curve of the bay and the sleepy blue and green ocean.

'Where are we, exactly?' he asked.

Ellie moved to stand next to him. 'On the False Bay coast. We're about twenty minutes from the CBD of Cape Town, to the south. That bay is False Bay and you can see about thirty kilometres of beach from here. Kalk Bay is that way—' she pointed '—and Muizenberg is up the coast.'

'What are those brightly coloured boxes on the beach?'

'Changing booths. Aren't they fun? The beach is hugely popular, and if you look just north of the booths, at the tables and chairs under the black and white striped awning, that's where we were—at Pari's.'

'It's incredible.'

'Your room looks out onto the beach and the bathroom has a view of the Muizenberg Mountain behind us. There are some great walks and biking trails in the nature reserve behind us.'

Ellie nudged one of two almost identical blond Labradors aside in an attempt to get close enough to the front door and shove her key in the lock. Pushing open the wooden door with its stained glass window insert, she gestured for Jack to come into the hall as she automatically hung her bag onto a decorative hook.

'The bedrooms are upstairs. I presume that you'd like a shower? Something to eat? Drink?'

He probably reeked like an abandoned rubbish dump. 'I'd kill for a shower.'

Jack had an impression of more bright colours and eclectic art as he followed Ellie up the wooden staircase. There was a short passage and then she opened the door to a guest bedroom: white and lavender linen on a double bed, pale walls and a ginger cat curled up on the royal purple throw.

'Meet Chaos. The *en-suite* bathroom is through that door.'

Ellie picked up Chaos and cradled the cat like a baby. Jack scratched the cat behind its ears and Chaos blinked sleepily.

Jack thankfully dropped his backpack onto the wooden floor and sat down on the purple throw at the end of the bed while he waited for the dots behind his eyes to recede. Ellie walked to the window, pulled the curtain back and lifted the wooden sash to let some fresh air into the room.

He dimly heard Ellie ask again if he wanted something to drink and struggled to respond normally. He was enormously grateful when she left the room and he could shove his head between his knees and pull himself back from the brink of fainting.

Because obviously he'd prefer not to take the concept of falling at Ellie's feet too literally.

Ellie skipped down the stairs, belted into the kitchen and yanked her mobile from her pocket.

Merri answered on the first ring. 'I know that you're upset with me about extending my maternity leave...'

'Shut up! This is more important!' Ellie hissed, keeping her voice low. 'Mitchell sent me a man!'

Merri waited a beat before responding. 'Your father is procuring men for you now? Are you *that* desperate? Oh, wait...yes, you are!'

'You are so funny...not.' Ellie shook her head. 'No, you twit, I'm acting as a Cape Town B&B for his stray colleagues again, but this time he sent me Jack Chapman!'

'The hottie war reporter?' Merri replied, after taking a moment to make the connection. She sounded awed and—gratifyingly—a smidgeon jealous. 'Well?'

'Well, what?'

'What's he like?' Merri demanded.

'He's reluctantly, cynically charming. Fascinating. And he has the envious ability to put people at ease. No wonder he's an ace reporter.' When low-key charm and fascination came wrapped up in such a pretty package it was doubly, mind-alteringly disarming.

'Well, well, well...' Merri drawled. 'It sounds like he has made *quite* an impression! You sound...breathy.'

Breathy? No, she did not!

But why did she feel excited, shy, nervous and—dammit—scared all at the same time? Oh, she wasn't scared of *him*—she knew instinctively, absolutely, that Jack was a gentleman down to his toes—but she was on a scalpel-edge because he was the first man in ages who had her nerve-endings humming and her sexual radar beeping. And if she told Merri *that*...

'You're attracted to him,' Merri stated.

She hated it when Merri read her mind. 'I'm not...it's just a surprise. And even if I was...'

'You are.'

'He's too sexy, too charming, has a crazy job that I loathe, and he'll be gone in a day or two.'

'Mmm, but he's seriously hot. Check him out on the internet.'

'Is that what you're doing? Stop it and concentrate!' She gave Merri—and herself—a mental slap. 'I have more than enough to deal with without adding the complication of even *thinking* about attraction and sex and a good-looking face topping a sexy body! Besides, I'm not good at relationships and men.'

'Because you're still scared to risk giving your heart away and having to take it back, battered and bruised, when they ride off into the sunset?'

Merri tossed her own words back at her and Ellie grimaced.

'Exactly! And a pretty face won't change anything. My father and my ex put me through an emotional grinder and Jack Chapman has the potential to do the same...'

'Well, that's jumping the gun, since you've just met him, but I'll bite. Why?'

'Purely because I'm attracted to him!' Ellie responded in a heated voice. 'It's an unwritten rule of my life that the men I find fascinating have an ability to wreak havoc in my life!'

They dropped in, kicked her heart around, ultimately decided that she wasn't worth sticking around for and left.

Merri remained silent and after a while Ellie spoke again. 'You agree with me, don't you?'

'No, don't take my silence for agreement; I'm just in awe of your crazy.' Merri sighed. 'So, to sum up your rant: you are such a bum magnet when it comes to men that your rule of thumb is that if you find one attractive then you should run like hell? Avoid at all costs?'

'You've nailed it,' Ellie said glumly.

'I want to see how you manage to do this when the man in question has moved his very hot self into your rather small house.'

Ellie disconnected her mobile on Merri's hooting laughter. Really, with friends like her...

Returning to the spare bedroom with towels for his bathroom and a cold beer in her hands, Ellie heard a low groan and peeked through the crack in the door to look at Jack, still sitting on the edge of the bed, his hands gripping the bottom of his shirt, pale and sweating.

Hurrying into the room, she dumped the towels on the bed, handed him the beer and frowned. 'Are you all right?'

Jack took a long, long drink from the bottle and rested the cold glass against his cheek. 'Sure. Why?'

'I noticed that you winced when you picked up your backpack. You took your time walking up the stairs, and now you're as white as a sheet and your hands are shaking!'

Jack rubbed the back of his neck. 'I'm a bit dinged up,' he eventually admitted.

'Uh-huh? How dinged up?'

'Just a bit. I'll survive.' Jack put the almost empty beer bottle on the floor and gripped the edge of his shirt again.

Ellie watched him struggle to pull it up and shook her head at his white-rimmed mouth.

'Can I help?' she asked eventually.

'I'll get there,' Jack muttered.

He couldn't, and with a slight shake of her head she stepped closer to the bed, grabbed the edges of his T-shirt and helped him pull it over his head. A beautiful body was there—somewhere underneath the blue-black plate-sized bruises that looked like angry thunderclouds. He had a wicked vertical scar bisecting his chest that suggested a major operation at one time, and Ellie bit her lip when she walked around his knees to look at his back. She couldn't stifle her horrified gasp. The damage on his back was even worse, and on his tanned skin she could see clear imprints of a heel here and the toe of a boot there.

'What does the other guy look like?' she asked, trying to be casual.

'Guys. Not as bad as me, unfortunately.' Jack balled his T-shirt in his hand and tossed it towards his rucksack. 'The Somalians decided to give me something to remember them by.'

Jack sat on the edge of the bed, bent over and, using one hand and taking short breaths, undid the laces of his scuffed trainers. When they were loose enough, he toed them off.

Jack sent her a crooked grin that didn't fool her for a second. 'As you can see, all in working order.'

'Anything broken?'

Jack shook his head. 'I think they bruised a rib or two. I'll live. I've had worse.'

Ellie shook her head. 'Worse than this?'

'A bullet does more damage,' Jack said, standing up and slowly walking to the *en-suite* bathroom.

Ellie gasped. 'You've been *shot*?'

'Twice. Hurts like a bitch.'

Hearing water running in the basin, Ellie abruptly sat down. She was instantly catapulted back in time to when she'd spent a holiday with Mitchell and his mother—her grandmother Ginger—in London when she was fourteen. He'd run to Bosnia to do a 'quick report' and come back in an ambulance plane, shot in the thigh. He'd lost a lot of blood and spent a couple of days in the ICU.

It wasn't her favourite holiday memory.

Jack didn't seem to be particularly fazed about his injuries; like Mitchell he probably fed on danger and adrenalin...it made no sense to her.

'You do realise that you could've died?' Ellie said, wondering why she even bothered.

Jack walked back into the room, dried his face on a towel he'd picked up from the bed and shrugged. 'Nah. They were lousy shots.'

Ellie sighed. She couldn't understand why getting hurt, shot or putting yourself in danger wasn't a bigger deterrent. She knew that Jack, like her father, preferred to work solo, shunning the protection of the army or the police, wanting to get the mood on the streets, the story from the locals. Such independence ratcheted up the danger quotient to the nth degree.

There was a reason why war reporting was rated as one of the most dangerous jobs in the world. Were they dedicated to the job or just plain stupid? Right now, seeing those bruises, she couldn't help but choose *stupid*.

'So, before I go...do you want something to eat?'

Jack shook his head. 'The pilot stood me a couple of burgers at the airport. Thanks, though.'

'Okay, well, I'll be downstairs if you need anything...' Ellie couldn't resist dropping her eyes to sneak a peek at his stomach. As she'd suspected, he had a gorgeous six-pack—but her attention was immediately diverted by a mucky, bloody sanitary pad held in place by the waist-band of his jeans.

She pursed her lips. 'And that?'

Jack glanced down and winced. With an enviable lack of modesty he flipped open the top two buttons of his jeans, pulled down the side of his boxer shorts and pulled off the pad. Ellie winced at the seeping, bloody, six-inch slash that bisected the artistic knife and broken heart tattoo on his hip.

'Not too bad,' Jack said, after prodding the wound with a blunt-edged finger.

'What is that? A knife wound?'

'Mmm. Psycho bastards.'

'You sound so calm,' Ellie said, her eyes wide.

'I *am* calm. I'm always calm.'

Too calm, she thought. 'Jack, it needs stitches.'

'This is minor, Ellie.' Jack looked mutinous. 'I'm going to give it a good scrub, slather it in the antiseptic I always carry with me and slap another pad on it.'

'Who uses sanitary pads for *this*?'

'It's an army thing and it serves the purpose. I'm an old hand at doctoring myself.'

Ellie sighed when Jack turned away to rummage in his rucksack. He pulled out another sanitary pad, stripped the plastic away and slapped the clean pad onto his still bleeding wound. She saw his stubborn look and knew that he'd made up his mind. If she couldn't get Jack to a hospital—he was six-two and built; how could she force him?—she'd have to trust him when he said that he was an old hand at patching himself up.

'When my bank cards arrive I'll go down to the pharmacy and get some proper supplies,' Jack told her.

Ellie sucked in a frustrated sigh. 'Give me a list of what you need and I'll run down and get it. I'll be back before you're finished showering.' She held up her hand. 'And, yes, you can pay me back.'

Jack looked hesitant and Ellie resisted the impulse to smack the back of his head. 'Jack, you need some decent medical supplies.'

Jack glared at the floor. She saw his broad shoulders dip in defeat before hearing his reluctant agreement. Within a minute he'd located a notebook from the side pocket of his rucksack and a pen, and he wrote in a strong, clear hand exactly what he wanted. He handed her the list and Ellie knew, by his miserable eyes, that he was embarrassed that he had to ask for her help. *Again.*

Men. Really...

The mobile in her pocket jangled and Ellie pulled it out, frowning at the unfamiliar number. Answering, she heard a low, distinctively feminine voice asking for Jack. Ellie's brows pulled together... How on earth could anyone know that Jack was with her? She had hardly completed that thought before realising that the jungle drums must be working well in the war journalists' world. Her father was spreading the news...

Ellie handed her mobile to Jack and couldn't help wondering who the owner of the low, subtly sexy voice was. Lover? Colleague? Friend?

'Hi, Ma.'

Or his mother. Horribly uncomfortable with the level of relief she felt on hearing that he was talking to his mother, Ellie scuttled from the room.

Jack lifted the mobile to his ear on an internal groan. He just wanted to go and lie down on that bed and sleep. Was that too much to ask? Really?

'I haven't been able to reach you for a week!' said his mother Rae in a semi-hysterical voice.

'Mum, we had an agreement. You only get to worry about me after you haven't spoken to me for three weeks.' Jack rubbed his forehead, actively trying to be patient. He understood her worry—after all that he'd put her and his father through how could he not?—but her over-protectiveness got very old, very quickly.

'Are you hurt?' his mother demanded curtly.

He wished he'd learnt to lie to her. 'Let me talk to Dad, Mum.'

'That means you're hurt. Derek! Jack's hurt!'

Jack heard her sob and she dropped the phone. His father's voice—an oasis of calm—crossed the miles.

'*Are* you hurt?'

'Mmm.'

'Where?'

Everywhere. There was no point whining about it. 'Couple of dents. Nothing major. Tell Mum to calm down to a mild panic.' Jack heard his mum gabbling in the background, listened through his father's reassurances and waited until his father spoke again.

'You mother says to please remind you to visit Dr Jance. Does she need to make an appointment for you?'

He'd forgotten that a check-up was due and he felt his insides contract. He did his best to forget what he'd gone through as a teenager, and these bi-yearly check-ups were reminders of those dreadful four years he'd spent as a slave to his failing heart. He tipped his head back in frustration when he heard Rae demand to talk to him again.

'Jack, the Sandersons contacted us last week,' she said in a rush.

Jack felt his heart contract and tasted guilt in the back of his throat. Abruptly he sat down on the edge of the bed. Brent Sanderson. He was alive because Brent had died. How could he *not* feel guilty? It was a constant—along with the feeling that he owed it to Brent to live life to the full, that living that way was the only way he could honour his brief life, the gift he'd been given...

'In six weeks it will be seventeen years since the op, and Brent was seventeen when he died,' Rae said with a quaver in her voice.

She didn't need to tell him that. He knew *exactly* how long it had been. They'd both been seventeen when they'd swapped hearts.

'They want to hold a memorial service for him and have invited us...and you. We've said we'll go and I said that I'd talk to you.'

Jack stretched out, tucked a pillow behind his head and blew out a long stream of air. He tried not to dwell on Brent and his past—he preferred the *it happened; let's move on* approach—and he really, really didn't want to go. 'It's a gracious invitation but I'm pretty sure that they'd be happy if I didn't pitch up.'

'How can you say that?'

'Because it would be supremely difficult for them to see me walking around, fit and healthy, knowing that their son is six feet under, Mum!'

They'd given him the gift of their son's heart. He'd do anything to spare them further pain. And that included keeping his distance...

'They aren't like that and they want to meet you. You've avoided meeting them for years!'

'I haven't avoided them. It just never worked out.'

'I'll pretend to believe that lie if you consider coming to Brent's service,' Rae retorted.

His mother wasn't a fool. 'Mum, I'll see. I've got to go. I'll visit when I'm back in the UK.'

'You're not in the UK? Where are you?' Rae squawked.

Jack gritted his teeth. 'You're mollycoddling me, and you know it drives me nuts!'

'Well, your career drives *me* nuts! How can you, after fighting so hard for life, routinely put yourself in danger? It's—'

'Crazy and disrespectful to take such risks when I've been given another chance at life. I'm playing Russian Roulette with my life and you wish I'd settle down and meet a nice girl and give you grandchildren. Have I left anything out?'

'No,' Rae muttered. 'But I put it more eloquently.'

'Eloquent nagging is still nagging. But I do love you, you old bat. Sometimes.'

'Revolting child.'

'Bye, Ma,' Jack said, and disconnected the call.

He banged the mobile against his forehead. His parents thought that guilt and fear fuelled his daredevil lifestyle. It did—of course it did—but did that have to be a bad thing? They didn't understand—probably because he could never explain it—but playing it safe, sitting behind a desk in a humdrum job was, for him, a slow way to die. At fourteen he'd gone from being a healthy, rambunctious, sporty kid to a waif and a ghost, his time spent either in hospital rooms or at his childhood home. He'd just *existed* for more years than he cared to remember, and he'd vowed that when he had the chance of an active life he'd live it. Hard and fast. He wanted to do it all and see it all—to chase the thrills. For himself and for Brent. Being confined to one house, person or city would be his version of hell. His parents wanted him to settle down, but they didn't understand that he wouldn't settle down for anything or anyone. He had to keep moving—and working to feel alive.

Jack switched off the bedside light and stared up at the shadows on the ceiling, actively trying not to think about his past. As per normal, his job had thrown him a curveball and he'd landed up in a strange bed in a strange town. But, he thought as his eyes closed, he was very good at curveballs and strange situations, and meeting Mitch's dazzling daughter again was very much worth the detour.

On his second night in Ellie's spare room, Jack put aside the magazine he'd been reading, rolled onto his back and stared at the ceiling above his bed. The air-conditioning unit hummed softly and he could hear the croaky song of frogs in the garden, the occasional whistle of a cricket. It wasn't that late and his side throbbed.

Knowing that he wouldn't be able to sleep yet, he flipped back the sheet and stood up. After yanking on a pair of jeans he quietly opened the door and walked to the stairs. Navigating his way through the dark house, he walked into the front lounge, with its two big bay windows, leaned against the side wall and looked through the darkness towards the sea. Through the open windows he could hear the thud of waves hitting the beach and smell the brine-tinged air.

Ellie's distinctively feminine voice drifted through the bay window, so he pulled back the curtain. He looked out and watched her walk up the stairs to the veranda, mobile to her ear and one arm full of papers and files. She looked exhausted and he could see flour streaks on her open navy chef's jacket. Jack glanced at the luminous dial of his watch...ten-thirty at night was a hell of a time to be coming home from work.

'Ginger, my life is a horror movie at the moment.'

Ginger? Wasn't that Mitchell's mother? Ellie's Irish grandmother?

'Essentially I need Mum to come back but it's not fair to ask her. I'm chasing my tail on a daily basis, it's nearly month-end, I have payroll and I need to pay VAT this month. And I need to move the bakery but there's nowhere to move it to! And, to top it all, your wretched son has sent me a house guest!'

So she wasn't as sanguine about having him as a guest as she pretended to be. Jack watched as she balanced the stack of papers and two files on the arm of the Morris chair.

'No, he's okay,' Ellie continued. 'I've had worse.'

Only okay? He was going to have to work on that.

Ellie used her free hand to dig into her bag for her house keys and half turned, knocking the unstable pile with her hip. The files tipped and the papers caught in the mild evening wind and drifted away.

'Dammit! Ginger—sorry, I have to go. I've just knocked something over.'

Ellie threw her mobile onto the seat of the Morris chair, then started to curse in Arabic. His mouth fell open. His eyes widened as the curses became quite creative, muddled and downright vulgar.

Jack thought that she could do with some help so he stepped over the sill of the low window directly onto the veranda and started to collect the bits of paper that were scattered all over the floor.

'Do you actually know what you're saying?' he demanded, when she stopped for ten seconds to take a breath.

Ellie sent him a puzzled look. 'Daughter of a donkey, son of a donkey, your mother is ugly, et cetera.'

Uh, no. Not even close. 'Do me a favour? Don't ever repeat any of those anywhere near an Arab, okay?'

Ellie slowly stood up and narrowed her eyes. 'They are rude, aren't they?'

He didn't need to respond because she'd already connected the dots.

'Mitchell! He taught me those when I was a kid.' It was so typical of Mitch's twisted sense of humour to teach his innocent daughter foul curse words in Arabic. 'I'm going to kill him! I take it you speak Arabic?'

'Mmm.' He'd discovered that he had a gift for languages while he was a teenager, when he'd been unable to do anything more energetic than read.

Ellie sent him a direct look. 'So, do you speak any other languages?'

Jack shrugged. 'Enough Mandarin to make myself understood. Some Japanese. I'm learning Russian. And Dari...'

'What's that?'

'Also known as Farsi, or Afghan Persian. Helpful, obviously, in Afghanistan.'

Ellie stared at him, seemingly impressed. 'That's incredible.'

Jack shrugged, uncomfortable with her praise. 'Lots of people speak second or third languages.'

'But not Farsi, Russian or Mandarin,' Ellie countered. 'I'm useless. I can barely spell in English.'

'I don't believe that.'

'You can ask Mitchell if you like. Nothing made him angrier than seeing my spelling test results,' Ellie quipped. 'Besides, English is a stupid language...their and there, which and witch, write, right, rite.'

'And another wright,' Jack added.

'You're just making that up,' she grumbled.

'I'm not. It's one of the few four-word homophones.' Jack's grin flashed. 'W.R.I.G.H.T. Someone who constructs or repairs things—as in a millwright.'

'Homophones? Huh.' Ellie heaved an exaggerated, forlorn sigh. 'Good grief, I'm sharing my house with a swot. What did I do to deserve that?'

Jack laughed, delighted. 'Life does throw challenges at one.'

After they'd finished collecting the papers Ellie sat down on the couch, rolling her head on her shoulders.

Jack sat on the low stone wall in front of her. 'Tough day?' he asked, conversationally.

Ellie slumped in the chair. 'Very. How can you tell?'

Jack lifted his hands. 'I heard you talking to your grandmother.'

'And how much did you hear?'

'You're pissed, you're stressed, something about having to move the bakery. You've had worse house guests than me.'

Even in the dim light he could see Ellie flush. 'Sorry. Mitchell tends to use me as his own personal B&B... I didn't mean to make you feel unwelcome.'

'Am I?'

Ellie threw her hands up and sent him a miserable look. 'You're not. I'm more frustrated at Mitchell's high-handedness than at the actual reality of a house guest, if that makes sense.'

Jack nodded, hearing the truth in her statement, and relaxed. 'Mitch does have a very nebulous concept of the word *no*,' he stated calmly.

'And he's had twenty-eight years to perfect the art of manipulating me,' Ellie muttered. 'Again, that's not directed at you personally.'

Jack laughed. 'I get it, Ellie. Relax. Talking about relaxing...' Jack walked back into the house, found a wine rack and remembered that he'd seen a corkscrew in the middle drawer when he was looking for a bread knife earlier. He took the wine and two glasses back to the veranda. 'If I ever saw a girl in need of the stress-relieving qualities of alcohol, it's you.'

'If I have any of that I'll fall over,' Ellie told him, covering a yawn with her hand.

'A glass or two won't hurt.' Jack yanked the cork out, poured the Merlot and handed her a glass.

Ellie took the glass from him and took the first delicious sip. 'Yum. I could drink this all night.'

'Then it would definitely hurt when you wake up.' After a moment's silence, he succumbed to his curiosity. 'Tell me what that conversation was about.'

Ellie cradled the glass in her hand and eyed Jack across the rim. Shirtless, and with bare feet, he was a delectable sight for sore eyes at the end of a hectic day. 'You're very nosy.'

'I'm a journalist. It's a job requirement. Talk.'

She wanted to object, to tell him he was bossy—which he was—but she didn't. Couldn't. She needed someone to offload on and maybe it would be easier to talk to a stranger who was leaving... When *was* he leaving? She asked him.

Jack grinned. 'Not sure yet. Is it a problem if I stay for another night or two? I like your house,' he added, and Ellie's glass stopped halfway to her mouth.

'You want to stay because you like my house? Uh... why?'

'Well, apart from the fact that we haven't yet talked about Mitch, it's...restful.' Jack lifted a bare muscled shoulder. 'It shouldn't be with such bright colours but it is. I like hearing the sea, the wind coming off the mountain. I like it.'

'Thanks.' Ellie took a sip of wine. It would be nice to know if he liked her as much as he liked her house, but since she'd only spent a couple of hours with him what could she expect? Ellie couldn't believe she was even thinking about him like that. It was so high school— and she had bigger problems than thinking about boys and their nice bodies and whether they liked her back.

Jack topped up her wine glass and then his. He squinted at the label on the bottle. 'This is a nice wine. Maybe I should go on a wine-tasting tour of the vineyards.'

'That's a St Sylve Merlot. My friend Luke owns the winery and his fiancée Jess does the advertising for the bakery.'

'And we're back full circle to your bakery. Talk.' Jack boosted himself up so that he sat cross-legged on the stone wall, his back to a wooden beam.

His eyes rested on her face and they encouraged her to trust him, to let it out, to *talk* to him...

Damn, he was good at this.

Ellie's smile was small and held a hint of pride. 'Pari's Perfect Cakes—'

'Who was Pari, by the way?' Jack interrupted her.

'My grandmother. It was her bakery originally. It means "fairy" in India.' Pain flashed in her eyes. 'As you saw, Pari's is a retail bakery and delicatessen, with a small coffee shop.'

'It doesn't look like a small operation. How do you manage it all?'

'Well, that's one of my problems. We have two shifts of bakers who make the bread and the high turnover items, and Merri, my best friend, used to do the specialised pastries. I do special function cakes. My mum did the books, stock and payroll and chivvied us along. It all worked brilliantly until recently.'

Jack held up his hand. 'Wait—back up. Special function cakes? Like wedding cakes?'

'Sure—but any type of cakes.' Ellie picked up her mobile and quickly pressed some buttons. 'Look.'

Jack put his glass of wine next to him on the wall and leaned forward to take the device. He flipped through the screens, looking at her designs.

'These are amazing, Ellie.'

'Thank you.'

He looked down at her mobile again. 'I can't believe that you made a cake that looks exactly like a crocodile leather shoe.'

'Not any shoe—a Christian Louboutin shoe.'

Jack looked puzzled. 'A what?'

'Great designer of shoes?' Ellie shook her head.

'Sorry, I'm more of a trainers and boots kind of guy.' Jack handed the mobile back to her. 'So, what went wrong at the bakery?'

'Not wrong, exactly. Merri had a baby and started her maternity leave. She told me yesterday that she's extending it.'

'She *told* you?'

Ellie heard the disbelief in Jack's voice and quickly responded, 'She asked...suggested...kind of.'

Jack frowned. 'And you said yes?'

'I didn't have much of a choice. She doesn't need to work and I didn't want to push her into a corner and...'

'And you couldn't say no,' Jack stated with a slight shake of his head.

'And I suppose you've never said yes when you wanted to say no?' Ellie demanded.

'I can't say that I've never done that. I generally say what I mean and I never let anyone push me around...'

'She didn't...' Ellie started to protest but fell silent when she saw the challenging expression on Jack's face. This wasn't an argument she would win because—well, she *did* get pushed around. Sometimes. Would he understand if she told him that, as grown-up and confident as she now was, she still had intense periods of self-doubt? Would he think her an absolute drip because her habit reaction was to make sure everyone around her was happy? And if they were they would love her more?

'What else?' Jack asked, after taking a sip of wine.

Ellie swirled the wine in her glass. 'My mother has taken a year's sabbatical. She always had this dream to travel, so for her fiftieth birthday I gave her a year off. A grand gesture that I am deeply regretting now. But she's in seventh heaven. She's got a tattoo, has had at least one affair and has put dreadlocks in her hair.'

'You sound more upset about the dreadlocks than the affair.'

Ellie shrugged. 'I just want her home—back in the bakery. She managed the place, did the paperwork and the accounts, the payroll and just made the place run smoothly.'

And while I say that I want everyone to be happy I frequently resent the fact that she left, that Merri left—okay, temporarily—and I have to carry on, pick up the pieces. When do I get to step away?

'So, you're stressed out and doing the work of two other people?'

'And none of it well,' Ellie added, her tone sulky.

Jack smiled. 'Now, tell me about having to move.'

Ellie gave him the rundown and cradled her glass of wine in her hands. She felt lighter for telling him, grateful to hand over the problem just for a minute. She didn't expect him to solve the problem, but just being able to verbalise her emotions was liberating.

And, amazingly, Jack just listened—without offering a solution, a way to fix it. If he wasn't ripped and didn't have a stubble-covered jaw and a very masculine package she could almost pretend he was a girlfriend. He listened like one. *Keep dreaming*, she thought. Not in a million years could she pretend that Jack was anything but a hard-ass—literally and metaphorically—one hundred per cent male.

Ellie yawned, curled her legs up and felt her eyes closing. She felt Jack take the glass from her hand and forced her eyes open.

'Come on. You're dead on your feet.' Jack took her hands and hauled her up.

He'd either overestimated her weight or underestimated his strength because she flew into his chest and her hands found themselves splayed across his pecs, warm and hard and...*ooooh*... Her nose was pressed against his sternum. She sucked him in along with the breath she took...man-soap, man-smell...*Jack*.

She felt tiny next to his muscled frame as his hands loosely held her hips, fingers on the top of her bottom. A lazy thumb stroked her hipbone through the chef's jacket and Ellie felt lust skitter along her skin. She slowly lifted her head and looked at him from beneath her eyelashes. There was half a smile on his face, yet his eyes were dark and serious...

He lifted his hand and gently rested his fingers on her lips. She knew what he was thinking...that he wanted to kiss her. Intended to kiss her.

Ellie just looked up at him with big eyes. She felt like a deer frozen in the headlights, knowing that she should pull away, unable to do so. She could feel his hard body against hers, his rising chest beneath her palms. His arms were strong, his shoulders broad. She felt feminine and dainty and...judging by the amount of action in his pants...desired.

He stepped back at the same time as she pushed him away. She shoved her hands into her hair, squinting at him in the moonlight. This was crazy... She was adult enough to recognise passion that could be perilous—wild, erratic and swamping. But lust, as she'd learnt, clouded her thinking and stripped away her practicality. Lust, teamed with the brief emotional connection she'd felt earlier, when she'd opened up a little to him, had her running scared.

Bum magnet.

Jack cocked his head. 'So, not a good idea, huh?'

Ellie bit her lip. 'Really not.'

Jack lifted a shoulder and sent her a rueful smile. 'Okay. But you're a very tempting sight in the moonlight so maybe we should go in before I try to change your mind.'

When she didn't move, Jack reached out and ran a thumb over her bottom lip.

'You can't just stand there looking up at me with those incredible eyes, Ellie. Go now, before I forget that I am, actually, a good guy. Because we both know that I could persuade you to stay.'

Ellie erred on the side of caution and fled inside.

THREE

——

EVERY TIME HIS foot slapped the pavement a hot flash of pain radiated from his cut and caused every atom in his body to ache. It was the morning after almost kissing Ellie, and he was dripping with perspiration and panting like a dog.

He placed his hand against his side and winced. He shouldn't be running, he knew that, but running was his escape, his sanity, his meditation. And, thinking about things he shouldn't be doing, kissing Ellie was top of the list. Why was he so tempted by his blue-eyed hostess? Especially since he'd quickly realised that she wasn't into simple fun and games, wasn't someone he could play with and leave, wasn't a superficial type of girl. And he didn't do anything *but* superficial.

But there was something about her that tweaked his interest and that scared the hell out of him.

He started to climb the hill back home and—dammit! He *hurt*. Everywhere. *Suck it up and stop being a pansy*, he told himself. *You've had a heart transplant—a cut and a beating is nothing compared to that!*

Jack pushed his wet hair off his forehead and looked around. Good Lord, it was beautiful here...the sea was aqua and hunter-green, cerulean-blue in places. White-yellow sand. Eclectic, interesting buildings. He was lucky to be here, to see this stunning part of the world...

Brent never would.

Brent never would. The phrase that was always at the back of his mind. Intellectually he knew it came from survivor's guilt—the fact that he was alive because Brent was dead. In the first few months and years after the op he'd been excited to be able to do whatever he wanted, but he knew that over the past couple of years the burden of guilt he felt had increased.

Why? Why wasn't he coming to terms with what had happened? Why wasn't it getting easier? The burden of the responsibility of living life for someone else had become heavier with each passing year.

The mobile he'd borrowed from Ellie jangled in his pocket and he came to an abrupt stop. Thankfully he was back at Ellie's place. He didn't think he could go any further.

'So, what do you think of Ellie?' Mitchell said when Jack pushed the green button on the mobile and held it up to a sweaty ear.

'Uh...she's fine. Nice.'

She was...in the best sense of the word. A little highly strung, occasionally shy. Sensitive, overwhelmed and struggling to hide it. Sexy as hell.

'So, have you talked to her about me yet?'

Jack lifted his eyebrows at Mitchell's blatant narcissism and felt insulted on Ellie's behalf.

'Ellie's well, but over-worked. Her bakery is fabulous; she's running it on her own as her mum is overseas,' he said, his tone coolly pointed as he answered the questions Mitch should have thought to ask.

'Yeah, yeah... But how far have you got with the book? Did you get my e-mail? I sent it just now.'

His verbal pricks hadn't dented Mitchell's self-absorbed hide. Jack wished he could reach into the phone and slap Mitchell around the head. Had he always been so self-involved? Why hadn't he noticed before? Jack sighed and looked at his watch. It wasn't quite seven yet. Far too early to deal with Mitchell.

'Firstly, my laptop is still in Somalia, and, contrary to what you think, I don't hover over my laptop waiting for your e-mails,' Jack said as he made his way into the house, up the steps and into his room. Jack heard Mitchell splutter with annoyance but continued anyway. 'And, by the way, why did you teach Ellie such crude Arabic insults when she was a little girl? They are, admittedly, funny as hell, because she gets them all mixed up, but really...'

'She still remembers those, huh?'

Jack pulled his T-shirt over his head, walked into the bathroom and dropped it into the laundry basket. Yanking a bottle of pills out of his toiletry bag, he shook the required daily dosage into his hand, tossed them into his mouth and used his hand as a cup to get water into his mouth.

Those pills were his constant companions, his best friends. He loved them and loathed them in equal measure.

'And why did you tell Ellie that I'm *helping* you write this book?'

As per normal, Mitch ignored the questions he didn't want to answer. 'So, have you spoken to Ellie yet about *me*?'

'No. The woman works like a demon. I haven't managed to pin her down yet.' Jack frowned. 'And she's not exactly jumping for joy at the prospect.'

Mitchell didn't answer for a minute. 'Ellie and I have had our ups and downs...'

Ups and downs? Jack suspected that they'd had a lot more than that.

'She didn't like me being away so much,' Mitchell continued.

Jack rolled his eyes at that understatement. As he walked over to the window his eye was caught by two frames lying against the wall, behind the desk in the corner. Pulling them out, he saw that they were two photographs of a younger Ellie and a short blond man in front of the exclusive art gallery Grigson's in London. Jack asked Mitch who the man in the photograph was.

'Someone she was briefly engaged to—five, six years ago.' Jack heard Mitchell light a cigarette. 'She wanted to get married. He didn't.'

Jack felt a spurt of sympathy for the guy. He'd had two potential-to-become-serious relationships in the past ten years and they'd both ended in tears on his partner's face and frustration on his. They'd wanted him to settle down. He equated that to being locked in a cage. He'd liked them, enjoyed them, but not enough to curtail his time or freedom for them.

'Jack? You still there?' Mitchell asked in his ear.

'Sure.'

'I spoke to most of our commissioning editors today and told them that you've been injured. They will leave you alone for three weeks. Unless something diabolical happens—then all bets are off,' Mitchell stated.

That was enough to yank his attention back, and fast. Jack felt his molars grinding. 'You do know I get very annoyed when you interfere in my life, Mitchell?'

Mitchell, never intimidated, just laughed. 'Oh, get over yourself! You haven't taken any time off in two years and we all know that leads to burnout. You've been flirting with it for a while, boyo.'

'Crap.'

'If you don't believe me, check your last couple of stories. You've always been super-fair and unemotional, but there's a fine line between being unemotional and robotic, Jack. You are drifting over that line. Losing every bit of empathy is every bit as problematic as having too much.'

'Again…crap,' Jack muttered, but wondered if Mitchell had a point. He remembered being in Egypt six weeks ago and watching a paramedic work on a badly beaten protester. He'd been trying to recall if he'd paid his gas bill. Maybe he was taking the role of observer a bit too far.

'I'm going to courier you my notebooks, my diaries,' Mitchell told him. 'Get some sun, drink some wine. But if you don't get cracking on my book…'

Mitch repeated the most gruesome of Ellie's Arabic curses from the night before and Jack winced.

Jack tossed the mobile onto the bed, slapped his hands on his hips and stared at the photographs he'd replaced against the wall. Ellie… Maybe he should think about leaving, and soon. Almost kissing her last night had been a mistake...

Sure, he was attracted to her—she was stunning; what man wouldn't be? If she was a different type of girl then he could have her, enjoy her and then leave. Unfortunately he wasn't just physically attracted, and he *knew* that mental attraction was a sticky quagmire best avoided. And, practically, while Mitch wouldn't win any Father of the Year awards he might not approve of them hooking up, and he didn't want to cause friction between him and his subject, mentor and colleague.

Ellie, with her cosy house and settled lifestyle—the absolute opposite of what he liked and needed—was also far more fascinating than he generally liked his casual partners to be. Because fascination always made leaving so much harder than it needed to be.

'Morning.'

Ellie jumped as he entered the kitchen, looking tough and rugged and a whole lot of sexy. She could see that his hair had deep red highlights in the chocolate-brown strands. He'd scraped off his beard and the violet stripes under his eyes were almost gone. He did, however, still have that glint in his eyes—the one that said he wanted to tear up the bedcovers with her.

Ellie cursed when she felt heat rising up her neck.

'Can I get some coffee?'

Jack's question yanked her out of her reverie and she nodded, reaching for a mug above the coffee machine to give her hands something to do.

'You're up early,' she said when she'd found her voice.

Jack took the cup she handed him and leaned against the counter, crossing his legs at the ankles. 'Mmm. Good coffee. I went for a run this morning along the beach-front. It was...absolutely amazing. It's such a beautiful part of the world.'

'It is, but should you be exercising yet?'

'I'm fine.'

Yeah, she didn't think so—but it was his body, his choice, his pain. Ellie shook her head, picked up her own cup and sipped. She echoed his stance and leaned against the counter. Tension swirled between them and Ellie thought she could almost see the purple elephant sit-ting in the room, eyebrow cocked and smirking.

Maybe it would be better just to get it out there and in the open. But she couldn't get the words out... How she wished she could be one of those upfront, ballsy girls who just said what they felt and lived with the consequences.

She was still—especially when it came to men—the shy, awkward girl she'd been as a teenager.

Jack's eyebrows pulled together. 'The wariness is back in your eyes. Why?'

'Uh...last night. Um—' Oh, great. Now her tongue was on strike.

Jack, no slouch mentally, immediately picked up on what she was trying to say. 'The kiss that never hap-pened?'

Ellie blushed. 'Mmm.'

'Yeah—sorry. I said I wouldn't hit on you and I did.' His tone didn't hold a hint of discomfort or embarrassment.

Ellie bit the inside of her lip. That wasn't what she'd expected him to say. Actually, she had no idea *what* she'd thought he'd say. The purple elephant grinned. 'I just... It's just that...'

Jack scratched the underside of his jaw and looked at her with his gold-flecked eyes. 'Relax, Ellie,' he said. 'It won't happen again...'

Ellie lifted her eyes to meet his and swallowed. In his she could read desire and lust and a healthy dose of amusement...as if he could read her thoughts, understand her confusion.

'Well...' he drawled as his finger gently pushed back a strand of hair that had fallen over her left eye. 'Maybe I should clarify that. I'll try not to let it happen again. You're very, very kissable, Ellie Evans.'

Ellie's eyes narrowed. She might not be the most assertive person in the world but that didn't mean he could look at her with those hot eyes and that smirky expression. Or presume that whatever happened between them would be solely *his* decision. Ellie narrowed her eyes, gripped the finger that had come to rest on her cheek and bent it backwards.

Hating personal confrontation, but knowing she needed to do this for the sake of her self-respect, she took a deep breath and forced the words out. 'There's only one person who will decide what happens between us and that will be me—not you.'

Jack grimaced and yanked his index finger out of her grip. He shook his finger out and sent her a surprised look. But, gratifyingly, there was an admiration in those hazel eyes that hadn't been there before and she liked seeing it there.

Jack sent her an approving smile. 'Good for you. I was wondering if you could stand up for yourself.'

Ellie narrowed her eyes. 'When I need to. No casual kissing.'

'Can we do *non*-casual kiss...?' Jack held up his hands at her fulsome glare. 'Joke! Peace!'

'Ha-ha.' Ellie rolled her shoulders. 'Would you like to go to work for me today?' she asked, blatantly changing the subject. 'I could do with a day off.'

'Okay—except my sugar icing and sculpting skills are sadly lacking. I can, however, make a mean red velvet cake.'

Ellie lowered her cup in surprise. 'You can bake?'

Ellie thought she saw pain flicker in his eyes. When he spoke his voice was gruff.

'Yes, I can bake. Normal stuff. Not pastries and croissants and fancy crap.'

Fancy crap? Well, that was one way to describe her business.

'Who taught you?' Ellie asked, openly curious.

'My mother.'

Ellie lifted her eyebrows. 'Sorry, I can't quite picture you baking as a kid. On bikes, on a sports field, camping—yes. Baking...no.'

Jack placed his cup on the counter and turned his face away from her. 'Well, it wasn't from choice.'

He sipped his coffee and when he looked at her again his face and eyes were devoid of whatever emotion she'd seen. Fear? Anger? Pain? A combination of all three?

This time it was Jack's turn to change the subject. 'So—breakfast. What are we having?'

Ellie looked at her watch and shook her head. 'No time. I need to go. I was supposed to be at work an hour ago.'

Jack shook his head. 'You should eat.'

'I'll grab something at the bakery.'

Well, she'd try to, but she frequently forgot. There just wasn't time most days. Ellie sighed. One of these days she'd have to start eating properly and sleeping more, but it wouldn't be any time soon. Maybe when Merri came back she could ease off a bit...but she probably wouldn't.

After all, she had a business to save.

Ellie looked at Jack, who was pulling eggs and bacon out of her fridge. Her mouth started to water. She'd kill for a proper fry-up...

Ellie pulled her thoughts away from food. 'So, I've given you keys to the house and I've just paid the deposit for you to hire a car. It should be delivered by eight so you won't be confined to the house any more.'

'The receipt for the deposit?' Jack sent her a level look.

Ellie rolled her eyes. He was insistent that she kept receipts for everything she spent so that he could repay her. 'In the hollow back of the wooden elephant on the hall table. With all the others.'

The annoying man wouldn't even allow her to buy milk or bread without asking for a receipt.

'Thanks.'

Jack slit open the pack of bacon and Ellie whimpered. She really, really didn't have time. She picked up her keys and bag, holding her chef's jacket in one hand.

'Pop down to the bakery later. I'll show you around. If you want to,' she added hastily.

Jack's smile had her melting like the gooey middle of her luscious chocolate brownies.

'I'll do that. See you later, then.'

Ellie bravely resisted the arc of sexual awareness that shimmered between them and sighed as she walked out of the kitchen.

In your dreams, Ellie. Because that was the only place making love to Jack was going to happen.

And even there her heart wasn't welcome to come to the party. Her heart, she'd decided a long time ago, wasn't allowed to party with *anyone* any more.

Later, dressed in denim shorts, flip-flops and an easy navy tee, Jack slipped through the front door of Pari's and looked over Ellie's business.

There were café-style tables outside, giving patrons the most marvellous view of the beach while they sipped their coffee and ate their muffins, and more wrought-iron tables inside, strategically placed between tables piled with preserves and organic wines, ten different types of olive oil and lots of other jars and tins of exotic foods with names he barely recognised. The décor was bohemian chic—he'd noticed that before—and all effortlessly elegant. Huge glass display fridges held a wide variety of pastries and cakes, and in another layer thick pink hams, haunches of rare roast beef and dark sausages.

It looked inviting and happy, and there was a line of people three deep at the wide counter, waiting to be served. The place was rocking, obviously extremely popular, and Jack suddenly realised what effort would be needed to move the bakery. If Ellie could find a place to move it to...

'Jack!'

Jack whipped his head up and saw Ellie approaching a table in the back corner of the room, a bottle of water in her hand. A good-looking couple sat at the table and Ellie motioned him over. Jack threaded his way through tables and people and ended up at the table, where a fourth chair was unoccupied.

'Paula and Will—meet my friend Jack. Take a seat, Jack,' Ellie said.

After shaking hands with Will, Jack pulled out the chair and sat down.

'I'm just about to chat to them about their wedding cake, but before we start does anyone want coffee?' Ellie continued.

Jack wasn't sure why he was sitting in on a client consultation, but since he didn't have anything better to do decided to go with the flow. He ordered a double espresso and noticed that Will was frowning at him.

'Do I know you?' Will asked, puzzled.

This was one of the things he most liked about Cape Town—the fact that people hardly recognised him. While he wasn't famous enough to attract paparazzi attention in the UK, his face was recognisable enough to attract some attention.

'I have one of those faces,' he lied.

Ellie sent him a grin. 'I'm just going to run through some ideas with Will and Paula, then I'll show you around.'

She placed her notebook on the table and switched into

work mode, outwardly confident. Jack listened as the couple explained why they now wanted a Pari's cake—their cake designer had let them down at the last moment—and watched, amazed, as Ellie took their rather vague ideas and transformed them into a quickly sketched but brilliantly drawn concept cake. He sampled various types of cake along with the couple, and when they asked for his opinion confirmed that he liked the Death by Chocolate best. Though the carrot ran a close second. Or maybe the fudge...

If he hung around the bakery more often Jack decided he'd have to add another couple of miles to his daily run to combat the calories and the cholesterol.

Ellie watched her clients go as she gathered her papers and shoved a pencil into the messy knot of hair behind her head.

'Today is Monday. Their wedding is on Saturday. I'm going to have to do some serious juggling to get it done for them.' Ellie rubbed her hand over her eyes.

'So why are you doing it, then?' Jack asked, curious.

'They are a sweet couple, and a wedding cake is important,' Ellie replied.

'Sweet? No. But they sure are slick.'

Ellie looked puzzled. 'What do you mean?'

She might be confident about her work but she was seriously naïve when it came to reading people, instinctively choosing to believe that people put their best foot forward.

Jack leaned his forearms on the table and shook his head. 'El, they were playing you.'

'What are you talking about?'

'They decided to come to you for their wedding cake—but it wasn't because their cake designer let them down. They knew there was no chance you'd make their cake at such late notice if they didn't have a rock-solid reason and they appealed to the romantic in you.'

'But why would you think that? I thought they were perfectly nice and above-board.'

'She doesn't blink—at all—when she lies, and his eyes slide to the right. Trust me, they were playing you.'

'Huh...' Ellie wrinkled her nose. 'Are you sure?'

Of course he was. He'd interviewed ten-year-olds with a better ability to lie. 'So, what are you going to do?'

Ellie stood up and shrugged. 'Make them their cake, of course. Let's go.'

Of course she was. Jack sighed as he followed her to the back of the bakery. She was going to produce a stunning, complicated cake in five days and their guests would be impressed, not knowing how she'd juggled her schedule to fit it in.

'I'm beginning to suspect you're a glutton for punishment,' Jack told Ellie as she pushed through the stable door leading to the back of the bakery. And a sucker too. But he kept that thought to himself.

She threw a look at him above her shoulder. 'Maybe—but did you notice that they didn't ask for a price?'

He hadn't, actually.

'And that order form they signed—at the bottom it states that there is a twenty-five per cent surcharge for rush jobs. Pure profit, Jack.'

Well, maybe not so much of a sucker.

Ellie walked over to a stainless steel table and tossed

her sketchpad onto it. She scowled at the design they'd decided on. 'There's a standard surcharge for rush jobs,' she admitted. 'But I really don't need the extra profit.'

'And now you're angry because they played you?' Jack commented.

'I was totally sucked in by Paula's big blue eyes, the panic I saw on her face. Will played his part perfectly as well, trying to reassure her while looking at me with those *help me* eyes!'

'They were good. Not great, but good.'

'*Arrgh!* I need the added pressure of making a wedding cake in five days like I need a hole in my head!'

'So call them up and tell them you can't do it,' Jack suggested.

That would mean going back on her word, and she couldn't do that. 'I can't. And, really, couldn't you have given me a heads-up *before* I agreed to make their damn cake?'

Jack cocked his head. 'How?'

'I don't know! You're the one who is supposed to be so street-wise and dialed-in... Couldn't you have whispered in my ear? Kicked my foot? Written me a damn note?'

Jack's lips quirked. 'My handwriting is shocking.'

'It is not. I've seen your writing!' Ellie shoved her hands into her hair. Her shoulders slumped. 'Useless man.'

'So I've been told.' He reached out and laid a hand on her shoulder, his expression suddenly serious. 'Sorry. It never occurred to me to interfere.'

She looked at him, leaning back against the wall, seemingly relaxed. But his eyes never stopped moving... He hadn't said anything to her because he was an observer.

He didn't get involved in a situation; he just commentated on it after the fact. She couldn't blame him. It was what he did. What journalists did.

She would have appreciated a heads-up, though. *Dammit.*

Ellie heard a high-pitched whistle and snapped her head up, immediately looking at the back section of the bakery, where the production area flowed into another room. Elias, one of her head bakers, stood at the wide entrance and jerked his head. Something in his body language had Ellie moving forward, and she reached her elderly staff member at the same time Jack did.

'What's wrong, Elias?' Ellie asked when she reached him.

Ellie felt Jack's hand on her lower back and was glad it was there.

Elias spoke in broken English and Ellie listened carefully. Before she had time to take in his words, never mind the implications, Jack was also demanding to know what the problem was.

'One of the industrial mixers is only working at one speed and the other one has stopped altogether,' she explained.

'That's not good,' Jack said.

'It's a disaster! We have orders coming out of our ears and we need cake. *Dammit!* Nothing happens in the bakery without the mixers... Elias, how did this happen?'

Elias shifted on his feet and stared at a point behind her head. 'I did tell you, Miss Ellie...the mixers...they need service. Did tell you...bad noise.'

Ellie scrubbed her face with her hands. He was right.

He *had* told her—numerous times—but she'd been so busy, feeling so overwhelmed, and the mixers had been working. It had been on her list of things to do but it had kept getting shoved to the bottom when, really, it should have been at the top.

Ellie placed her hands over her face again and shook her head. What was she going to do?

When she eventually dropped her hands she saw that Elias was walking out of earshot. Jack had obviously signalled that they needed some privacy. He placed his hands on the mixer and lifted his eyebrows at Ellie.

'Dropped the ball on this one, didn't you?' he remarked.

Ellie glared at him, her blue eyes laser-bright. 'In between juggling the orders and paying the staff and placing orders for supplies, I somehow forgot to schedule a service for the mixers! Stupid me.' She folded her arms across her chest as she paced the small area between them.

'It was, actually, since this is the heartbeat of your business.'

Did he think she didn't know that? 'I messed up. I get it... It's something I'm doing a lot lately.'

'Stop feeling sorry for yourself and start thinking about how you're going to fix the problem,' Jack snapped.

She felt the instinctive urge to slap him...slap *something*.

'You can indulge in self-pity later, but right now your entire production has stopped and you're wasting daylight.'

His words shocked some sense into her, but she reserved the right to indulge in some hysterics later. 'I need to get someone here to fix these mixers...' Ellie saw him shake his head and she threw up her hands. 'What have I said wrong now?'

'Priorities, Ellie. What are you going to do about your orders?'

'You mean the mixers,' Ellie corrected him.

Jack shook his head and reached for the paper slips that were stuck on a wooden beam to the right of the mixers. 'No, I mean the orders. Prioritise the orders and get...what was his name...Elias...to start hand-mixing the batter for the cakes that are most urgent.'

That made sense, Ellie thought, reluctantly impressed.

Ellie took the slips he held out and a pen and quickly prioritised the orders. 'Okay, that's done. I'll get him working on these.'

Jack nodded and looked at the mixers. 'Are these under guarantee or anything?'

'No. Why?'

'Got a toolbox?'

'A toolbox? Why? What for?'

'While Elias starts the hand-mixing I'll take a look at these mixers. I know my way around machines and motors. It's probably just a broken drive belt or a stripped gear.'

'Where on earth would you have learnt about machines and motors?' Ellie demanded, bemused.

'Ellie, I spend a good portion of my life in Third World countries, on Third World roads, using Third World transportation. I've broken down more times in more crappy cars than you've made wedding cakes. Since I'm not the type to hang about waiting for someone else to get things working, I get stuck in. I can now, thanks to the tutelage of some amazing bush mechanics, fix most things.'

Ellie shut her flapping mouth and swallowed. 'Okay, well...uh...there's a basic toolbox in the storeroom and a hardware store down the road if you need anything else.'

Jack put his hands on his hips. 'And get on that phone and get someone here to service those mixers. I might be able to get them running but they'll still need a service.'

Ellie looked at him, baffled at this take-charge Jack. 'Jack—thank you.'

'Get one of the staff to bring me that toolbox, will you?' Jack crouched on his haunches at the back of one of the machines and started to work off the cover that covered the mixer's motor. 'Hell, look at this motor! It's leaking oil...it's clogged up...when was this damn thing last serviced?'

Ellie, who thought that Jack wouldn't appreciate hearing that she hadn't the faintest clue, decided to scarper while she could and left Jack cursing to himself.

FOUR

——

ELIAS LAUGHED WHEN Jack messed up the traditional African handshake—again—and slapped him on the shoulder. 'We'll teach you yet, *mlungu*.'

'Ma-lun-goo?' Jack tested the word out on his tongue.

'"White man" in Xhosa,' said the old Xhosa baker.

'Ah.' Jack stared at Elias and a slow grin crossed his face. 'I heard you talking Xhosa earlier. I love the clicking sound you make. If I were staying I would want to learn Xhosa.'

'If you stay...' Elias grinned '...I teach you.'

'There's a deal,' Jack said, before bidding him goodnight and turning back to the rear entrance of the bakery.

Ellie looked up as he walked towards her and ran the back of her hand over her forehead. 'Bet you're regretting ambling down the hill this morning,' she said with a grateful smile.

'It's been an...interesting day,' Jack said, conscious of a dull headache behind his eyes. 'A baptism by grease, flour, sugar and baking powder...'

'I never expected you to help with either the fixing or the mixing, but thank you.'

He'd resurrected one of the mixers, and when a part arrived for the other mixer in the morning he'd have that up and running within an hour. While he'd been working on the mixers he'd watched Elias and his assistant falling further and further behind on the orders, and had instantly become their best friend when he'd got the one mixer working.

'Elias really battled physically to do that hand-mixing.'

Ellie cocked her head. 'So that's why you stepped in to help him?'

He shrugged. 'I thought he was going to have a heart attack,' Jack admitted.

He'd mixed the batter for more than a hundred and twenty cupcakes and, under Elias's beady eye, also mixed the ingredients for two Pari's Paradise Chocolate cakes and more than a few vanilla sponge cakes. His shoulders ached and his biceps were crying out for mercy...

'He's stronger than he looks. He should've retired years ago, but he doesn't want to and I can't make him.' Ellie sighed. 'He's worked here since the day the bakery opened. It's his second home, and as long as he wants to work I'll let him. But maybe I should try to sneak in another assistant.'

'Sneak in?'

'It took me six months to get him to accept Gideon in his space.' Ellie grinned. 'He's a wonderful old gent but he has the pride of Lucifer. I'm surprised he let you do anything.'

'Yeah, but I *did* get his beloved mixer working.'

'That you did,' Ellie agreed. 'And I'm so grateful. You worked like a dog today.'

Which raised the question...*why* had he bust his gut to help this woman he barely knew? He was an observer, not a participator, and her bakery wouldn't have gone into bankruptcy if they'd waited for a mechanic to fix the mixers. But he'd felt compelled to step up and get stuck in, to help her, to...

Aargh! He must have taken a blow to the head along with the stabbing and the beating, because this wasn't how he normally rolled.

Jack, frustrated at not recognising himself, thought that he'd kill for a beer or two. He stood next to Ellie's table and leaned his shoulder against a wall, watching her work. She'd been in the bakery for nearly twelve hours and she was still working on another cake. The nightshift of two more bakers were starting their shift and Ellie would probably be there to see them off in the morning.

She might tend to panic when she hit a snag but he admired her work ethic.

And her legs... Who would've thought that a chef's jacket over shorts and long tanned legs could look so sexy? Jack swallowed, uneasy at the realisation that he wanted...no, *craved* her.

He'd never had this reaction to any woman before. Generally it was easy come, easy go. Nothing about Ellie so far had been easy, and he suspected that nothing would be. Jack shifted on his feet as desire flared. It would be easy to seduce her, but that would make leaving in a couple of days that much more complicated. Because somehow he instinctively knew that he couldn't treat her as a casual encounter. There was something about Ellie that tugged at him—some button that she pushed that made him suspect that this was a woman worth getting to know...

And that was more terrifying than being caught in the crossfire in any hot zone anywhere in the world. They had yet to make flak jackets to protect against emotional bullets.

Ellie looked up from the bare cake in front of her, which had been cut into the vague shape of a train and was covered in rough white icing. She sent him a tired smile. 'I'm wondering what I can give you for supper.'

Jack pried himself off the wall and walked away from the table she was working at. 'Something simple...let's order pizza.'

Ellie sighed and Jack saw relief flicker on her face.

'Okay. I just need to finish this and we can go home. Or you can go home and I'll follow in a bit.'

Jack hooked a stool with his foot and rolled it towards him, sinking down onto it with a groan. 'I'll wait for you.'

Ellie pulled out a ball of fire-engine-red dough from a container and started to knead it with competent hands.

Jack stretched out his legs. 'What are you making with that red dough?'

'It's not dough. It's fondant icing. It's for a train cake,' Ellie explained. She gestured to what looked like a big pasta roller on the table next to hers. 'It goes in there to flatten it out, then I'll drape it over the cake.'

'Does it have to be done tonight?'

'It should be. Luckily, I can make this in my sleep.' Ellie

slapped her hand into the fondant and caught his look. 'What? Why are you looking at me like that?'

'I was just thinking about your business, what you do here.' He hadn't been, but he suspected that she wasn't ready to hear what he'd really been thinking...which involved her being naked and sliding all over him.

Oh, Lordy-be, there was that smile that made her womb vibrate. It was a combination of schoolboy naughtiness and sex-on-a-stick, and Ellie thought that stronger women than her would have trouble resisting it. She opened her mouth to ask what he was smiling about and practically bit her tongue in half to keep the words from escaping.

The hell of it was that while she'd initially thought that Jack might be all flash, today he had proved that he was more than just a hot body with a reasonably sharp brain. How many men of her acquaintance would have jumped in to help, tinkering with a motor and getting splattered with grease and then patiently mixing endless batches of batter—a thankless, back-breaking, horrible job to do by hand—without a word of complaint?

Ellie smoothed icing over the front of the train. The ability to give without asking for something in return, to jump into a situation and offer help when it was most needed, was a rare quality and unfortunately deeply attractive. Even more so than his hot body and masculine face.

Ellie's hand stilled on the cake as a panicked thought jumped into her head. She wanted him to go—now—tonight. She wanted him to go before she started imagining him in her bakery, in her life...before she started dreaming of a clear mind to keep her focused, a steady hand to prod her along, a hard body to touch and taste, then to curl up against at night.

Ellie fisted her hand and had to stop herself from punching the cake. She was suddenly ridiculously, outrageously angry at herself. Why was she even letting thoughts like those into her head? Considering what-ifs and maybes? Yes, he was a good-looking guy who gave her a buzz, a man nice enough to help her out, but there was no call to start thinking that he was anything more than a transient visitor. He was nothing but her father's friend, a brief acquaintance, and realistically she wasn't his type.

Oh, she was attractive enough for a brief fling, but she wasn't stupid enough to believe that she could ever be more than that. *Nobody will give up their freedom and time for monogamy with you...*

Jack had got up, rested his hand on her clenched fist and forced her fingers open.

Ellie twisted her lips and blew out a breath, but kept her eyes fixed on the cake.

'I think that's enough for now. We need pizza and beer and to chill,' he said.

Ellie pulled her hand out from beneath his and brushed her hair off her forehead with the tips of her fingers, leaving a trail of red icing on her forehead. 'This cake...'

'Will still be here tomorrow.' Jack took her hand again and pulled her away from the table. He leaned forward and his voice was low, seductive and sexy in her ear. 'Beer. Pizza.'

Ellie looked at the half-white, half-red train. Beer,

pizza and conversation with an interesting man versus a stupid train cake...? No contest.

The woman amazed him, Jack thought. Twenty minutes ago Ellie had looked as if she was about to collapse, but now, sitting across from him at a table on the deck of an admittedly fake, slightly scruffy Italian restaurant, she looked sensational. She'd pulled her hair back into a sleek ponytail which highlighted her amazing cheekbones and painted her lips a glossy soft pink. She'd sorted out the smudged make-up around her eyes and she looked and smelled as if she'd just stepped out of a shower.

He, on the other hand, felt as if he'd spent the day hauling hay and cleaning out stables. He took a long sip of his beer and sighed as the bittersweet liquid slid down his throat. The night was warm, the surf was pounding, he had a beer in his hand and a pretty girl across the table from him.

The only scenario that sounded better was if he'd had pizza in his belly and the girl was naked beneath him.

'There's that smile again,' Ellie murmured.

'Huh? What smile?'

Ellie rested her chin in the palm of her hand. 'You get this secretive, naughty, sexy smile...'

'Sexy?' The light on the deck was muted but Jack grinned as he saw her blush.

'Yeah, well...anyway. So, I'm starving.' Ellie looked around, not trying to hide the fact that she was looking to change the subject. 'Where's that pizza?'

Jack decided to let her off the hook—mostly because

flirting caused his pants to wake up and start doing its happy dance.

He looked around and narrowed his eyes. 'Have you had any more thoughts about the bakery?'

Ellie wrinkled her nose. She took a sip from her glass of wine and glanced at the ocean. 'Moving it, you mean?'

'Mmm.'

'I have an idea that I'm working on,' Ellie said mysteriously.

His curiosity was instantly aroused. 'You can't leave me hanging!' Jack protested when she didn't elaborate.

Ellie smiled. 'There might be a property that could work.'

'You don't have much time,' Jack pointed out.

'I know. Six months.'

Under the table Jack felt Ellie crossing her legs and he heard her sigh.

'I want to hyperventilate every time I think about it.'

'Call your mother and tell her to come home. It's her business too, El. You don't have to carry this load alone. Tell her about having to move. Tell her that you need help.'

'I can't, Jack. She's been working in that bakery for ever, never taking time off. Now she's living her dream and having such a blast. I can't ask her to give that up. Not just yet. And...and I feel that if I do I'm admitting failure. That I need my mummy to hold my hand.'

Jack shook his head. 'So you'd rather work yourself to a standstill, knocking yourself out, instead of asking your friend to come back to work and your mother to come back and help you?'

'Making sure that the people I love are happy is very important to me, Jack.'

'Not if it comes at too high a price to *you*.'

She'd inherited Mitchell's irritable, don't-mess-with-me stare.

'You're really sexy when you're irritated,' he commented idly, unfazed.

'I suspect that you can be annoying...' she paused for a beat and bared her teeth at him '...all the time.'

Jack grinned at her attempt to intimidate him. She looked as scary as a Siamese cat with an attitude disorder.

Ellie rubbed her temple with her fingertips. 'Can we not talk about the bakery tonight? I'd like to pretend it's not there for five minutes.'

Jack agreed and sighed in relief when he saw a waiter heading their way with pizzas. It wasn't a moment too soon. He thought his stomach was about to eat itself.

'So, why war reporting?' Ellie asked, when they'd both satisfied their immediate hunger.

Ellie wound a piece of stray cheese around her finger and popped it into her mouth. Jack nearly choked on the bite of pizza he'd just taken. *Hell...* He quickly swallowed and pulled his mind out of the bedroom. She was getting harder and harder to resist. And he *had* to resist her... mostly because she *was* so damn hard to resist.

Ellie repeating her question wiped the idea of sex—only temporarily, he was sure—from his brain.

'When I was about fifteen I watched a lot of news, and Mitch and other war reporters were reporting from Iraq. I was fascinated. They seemed larger than life.'

'He was. Is.'

'Then he was interviewed and he spoke about the travelling and the adrenalin and I thought it was a kick-ass career.' Jack bit, swallowed and grinned. 'I still think it is.'

Ellie's eyes were a deep blue in the candlelight and Jack felt as if she could see into his soul.

'How do you deal with the bad stuff you've seen? The violence, the suffering, the madness, the cruelty? How do you process all of that?'

Jack carefully placed his slice of pizza back down on his plate. He took a while to answer, and when he did he was surprised to hear the emotion in his voice. 'It took some time but I've programmed myself to just report on the facts. My job is to tell the story—hopefully in a way that will facilitate change. I observe and I don't judge, because judgement requires an emotional involvement.'

'And you don't get emotionally involved,' Ellie said thoughtfully. 'Does that carry over into other areas of your life?'

Jack stiffened, wondering where she was going with that question. 'You mean like relationships and crap like that?'

'Yeah—crap like that.' Ellie's response was bone-dry.

He had to set her straight. Right now. Just in case she had any ideas...

'Like your father, my life doesn't lend itself to having a long-term relationship. Women tend to get annoyed when you don't spend time with them.'

'Yep, I know what that feels like. Any woman who gets involved with a war reporter is asking to put her emotions through a meat-grinder,' Ellie replied. 'God knows that's exactly what Mitchell did to me.'

She didn't give him time to respond and was frustrated when she changed the subject.

'So, how is the book coming along?'

Ellie pushed her plate away and Jack frowned. She'd barely managed to eat half her medium pizza and he had almost finished his large. 'Well, apart from the fact that I can't get a certain reporter's daughter to sit down and answer my questions, fine.'

He saw guilt flash across her face. 'Oh, Jack, I'm so sorry! You probably want to leave, head home, and I'm holding you up—'

Jack shook his head. Where did this need to blame herself for everything come from? She was so together and confident in some ways—such a train wreck when it came to her need to please.

'Ellie, stop it!' Ellie's mouth snapped shut and Jack thought that was progress. 'Firstly, if I wanted to leave I would've made a plan to go already. Secondly, as I said, I like your house, I like this area, and when I start feeling pressurised for time I'll tell you and we'll get down to it. As long as you do not want me out of your house we're good. *Do* you want me to leave?'

'No, you're reasonably well house-trained,' Ellie muttered.

Jack grinned.

'So, why aren't you prepared to write your story? Mitchell said that you were asked to.' Ellie picked up the thread of their conversation again.

Because my story isn't just my story and it's a lot more complicated than people think. Jack swallowed those words and just shrugged.

Ellie picked an olive off her pizza and popped it into her mouth. They sat in a comfortable silence for a while, until Ellie spoke again. 'I think I know why you are reluctant to tell your story.'

This should be good. A little armchair analysis. 'Really? Why?'

'In light of what you said earlier, digging into your own story, analysing your life choices, would require emotional involvement. You can't stand back and just observe your own life. You can't be objective about yourself. Then again, who can?'

It was Jack's turn to stare at her, to feel the impact of her insightful words. He couldn't even begin to start formulating an argument. There wasn't one, because her observation was pure truth.

Jack drained the last inch of beer in his bottle and threw his serviette onto the table. 'You ready to go?'

Ellie nodded, pushed her chair back and pulled her purse out of her bag. He ground his teeth as she placed cash under the heavy salt cellar. Where the hell were his new bank cards? He was sick of not having access to funds.

He stopped at the cashier on the way out and asked for a receipt, and he knew without looking at Ellie that she was rolling her eyes at him.

'Jack, you worked in the bakery. I'll pay for dinner.'

'No.' Jack took the printed bill from the manager and shoved it into his pocket.

'Stop being anal.'

Jack gripped her ponytail and tugged gently. 'Stop nagging. I thought we agreed that if I'm living in your house then I'll pick up the tab?'

She tossed her head. 'We never agreed on anything!'

Jack's grin flashed. 'It's easier if you just do it my way.'

'In your dreams.'

It was shortly after six the following evening when Jack returned from a trip to Robben Island, the off-coast prison that had housed Nelson Mandela for twenty-four years, and his mind was still on the beloved South African icon when he walked into Ellie's kitchen.

He kicked off his shoes, dumped the take-away Chinese he'd picked up on the way on the kitchen table and tossed his brand-new wallet containing his brand-new bank cards onto the table. Inside was enough cash to reimburse Ellie for everything she'd paid for so far. Thinking about Ellie, he wondered where she was.

Jack walked back into the hall and stood at the bottom of the stairs, calling her name. Her bag was on its customary hook and her mobile sat on the hall table. Jack walked back to the kitchen, onto the back deck, and finally found her, sprawled out on a lounger in the shade of one of the two umbrellas that stood next to her pool.

She was asleep, with an open sketchbook on her bare, flat stomach and a piece of charcoal on the grass below her hand. She was dressed in a tiny black and blue bikini and he spent many minutes examining her nearly-but-not-quite naked body. Her long damp hair streamed over her shoulders and across the triangles that covered her full breasts. She had a flat, almost concave stomach, slim hips and long, smooth legs with fine muscles. The tips of her elegant feet were painted a vivid pink that reminded him of Grecian sunsets.

Very alluring, very sexy, Jack thought, sinking to the grass next to her chair. In order to stop himself from undoing those flimsy ties keeping those tiny triangles in place, he picked up the sketchpad and flipped through the pages.

The sketches were rough, jerky, but powerful, full of movement. She'd sketched her house, capturing its fat lines and bay windows, and there was a sketch of her dog, head on paws, his eyes soulful. There was a rather bleak landscape of cliffs and shadows which oozed sadness and regret.

Jack gasped at his likeness, grinning up at him from another white page. She'd captured his laugh and, worse, the attraction to her he'd thought he was hiding so well.

'Snoop.'

Jack snapped the book closed and looked up into her face. Her eyes were still closed and her eyelashes were ink-black on her face.

'I thought you were still asleep. I was trying to be quiet.'

'I'm a really light sleeper,' Ellie said, and held out her hand for her sketchpad.

Jack reluctantly handed it over. 'These are good—'

'It's something I do to pass the time.' Ellie tossed the pad on top of a box of charcoal sticks and sat up, covering her mouth as she yawned. 'Talking of which, what *is* the time?'

Jack looked at his watch. 'Half-six.'

Ellie looked horrified. 'I went for a swim around five

and thought I'd take fifteen minutes to chill... I must've dozed off.'

Jack drew his thumb across the purple shadow under her eye. 'It looks like you needed it. What time did you finish last night? I saw your light was still on after midnight.'

'One? Half-one? I finished the VAT return and paid some creditors.' Ellie swung her legs off the sunchair, her feet brushing Jack's thighs. 'I've got a couple of hours' work tonight and then I'll be caught up. I shouldn't have fallen asleep...I meant to work after my swim.'

Jack clenched his fists in an effort not to reach for her. She looked so tired, so young, so...*weary* that all he wanted to do was take her in his arms and ease her stress. He shoved his hand into his hair. *She tries to hide it*, he thought, *but she's wiped out in every way she can be by the responsibilities of her business.* He wished there was something he could do for her. Dammit, was he starting to feel protective over her? He didn't know how to handle her, deal with her. He was used to resilient, emotionally tougher women, and Ellie had him wanting to shield her, shelter her.

'I need to think about what to make for supper,' Ellie said as she stood up, unfurling that long, slender body.

Her voice was saturated with exhaustion and he felt irritation jump up into his throat. 'Ellie, I am *not* another one of your responsibilities!' he snapped.

Ellie blinked at him. 'You don't want me to make supper?'

'No. For a number of reasons. The first being that I bought supper—Chinese. My replacement bank cards arrived,' he explained when she looked at him enquiringly.

'Also, I really think you need to learn that the world will not stop turning if you stop for five minutes and relax. You never stop moving, and when you do you're so exhausted that you can't keep your eyes open.'

Ellie picked up a sarong and wound it around her hips. 'Jack, please. I really don't want to argue with you.'

Jack nodded. 'Okay, I won't argue. I'll just tell you what to do. You're going to change into something that doesn't stop traffic and then we're going for a walk. On the way we'll stop and have a beer at one of the pubs on the beachfront. Then we'll come home, eat Chinese, of which you will have a reasonable portion, and then you're going to bed. Early.'

'Jack, it's hot. I don't feel like a walk and I can't take the time—'

'Yeah, you can,' Jack told her. 'And I know you're hot. You're standing there in a couple of triangles cooking my blood pressure. So this should help both of us cool off.'

Jack scooped her up, ignored her squeal and stepped, still dressed, into the deep end of her gloriously cold, sparkling blue pool.

FIVE

'IT'S SUCH A stunning evening. Would you like to take the long route to the beachfront?' Ellie asked him as they stepped onto the road outside her house. 'It's a ten-minute walk instead of a five-minute walk but I'll show you a bit of the neighbourhood.'

'Sure,' Jack agreed, and they turned left instead of right.

He walked next to Ellie, his hands loose in the pockets of his shorts. The sea in front of them was pancake-flat and a patchwork quilt of greens and blues. It was make-your-soul-bump beautiful. The temperature had dropped and she was cool from the swim and the light, short sundress she was wearing.

She was really looking forward to an icy margarita and Jack's stimulating, slightly acerbic company.

A little way away from the house Jack broke their comfortable silence. 'By the way, I was contacted today by the Press Club. They've heard that I'm in town and have invited me to their annual dinner. I'd like you to go with me, but I know how busy you are. Any chance?'

Ellie's heart hiccupped. A date! A real date! *Whoop!* She did an internal happy dance. 'When is it?'

'Tomorrow. Tomorrow *is* Friday, right? It's black tie, I'm afraid.'

A date where she could seriously glam up? Double *whoop!*

'So, do you think you can leave work early for a change?' Jack enquired. 'It's a hassle going to these functions on my own.'

In a strange city where he knew no one of course it would be. And the world wouldn't stop turning if she left work a little earlier than normal. Besides, Merri would come in for an hour or two.

'Sure. That sounds like fun.'

'Great.' Jack moved between her and a large dog that was walking along the verge of a house with its gates left open.

Ellie appreciated his innate protectiveness but she knew Islay. He was as friendly as he was old.

Jack cleared his throat. 'Ellie, I was only supposed to spend one, maybe two nights in your house...'

'And tonight will be your fourth night,' Ellie replied quietly. 'Do you want to leave?'

Jack shook his head. 'Just the opposite, actually. Mitch, being Mitch, has put the word out to the network editors that I'm hurt and need some time off.'

Ellie flicked a glance at his hip. 'You *are* hurt.'

'Superficially.' Compared to what he'd gone through, his stab wound was minimal. 'Anyway, I'm off for a few weeks unless—'

She knew the drill. Journalists were only 'off' until the next story came along. 'Unless some huge story breaks.'

Jack nodded his agreement. 'So, I thought I'd stay in Cape Town for a bit longer.'

'In my house?' Ellie heard the squeak in her voice and winced. She sounded like a demented mouse.

'Well, I could move into a hotel, but I spend enough time in hotels as it is and I'd rather pay you.'

Ellie stopped in her tracks and turned to look at him. 'You'd pay to live with me?'

What exactly did he mean by that? What would be included in that deal? Not that she believed for one minute that he'd make her an offer that was below-board, but she just wanted to make sure... And really, how upset would she be if he suggested sleeping together? Since she was constantly thinking about sex with him...not very.

His grin suggested he knew exactly what she was thinking. 'It's a simple transaction, Ellie. Someone has to get paid to put my butt into a bed and I'd prefer it to be you and not some nameless, faceless corporation.' Jack stepped forward and his thumb drifted over her chin. 'A bed, food, coffee. No expectations, no pressure.' Damn.

'Oh.' Ellie dropped her head and thought she was an idiot for feeling disappointed. *You don't want to get involved, on any level, with any man—remember, Ellie?* Especially a man like Jack. Too good-looking, too successful, too much. Rough, tough, unemotional and—the big reason—never around.

But she wanted him. She really did.

Jack dropped his hand and Ellie was glad, because she didn't know for how much longer she could stop herself reaching up and kissing him, tasting those firm lips, feeling the rasp of his stubble under her lips, her fingers. She watched him walk away and after two steps he turned and looked back at her.

He must have seen something on her face, because his steps lengthened and then his hands were on her hips, yanking her into him. His mouth finally touched hers sweetly, gently, before he allowed his passion to explode. His quick tongue slipped between her lips, scraped her teeth and tangled with her own in a long, deep kiss that had no end or beginning.

One hand held her head in place and the other explored her back, her hip, the curves of her bottom, the tops of her thighs. Ellie slid her hand up his back, under his loose T-shirt, and acquainted herself with his bare flesh, the muscles in his back, that strip of flesh above his shorts and the soft leather belt. He was heat and lust and passion in its purist, most concentrated form; causing her nipples and her thighs to press together to subdue the deep, insistent throbbing between them.

He kissed her some more.

Ellie wasn't sure how much time had passed when he finally lifted his head and rested his forehead against hers. 'I'm burning up, on fire from wanting you. That's why I haven't kissed you before this.'

'Why did you kiss me now?' Ellie whispered back, her hands gripping his sides.

'Because you looked like you wanted me to—really wanted me to.'

She really had. And she wouldn't object to more.

Jack stepped back, linked his hands behind his head.

The muscles in his arms bulged. 'I can't take you to bed...
I mean of course I *can*. I want to. Desperately. But it would
be the worst idea in the world.'

It didn't matter that she agreed with him. She wanted
to know why he thought so. 'Why?'

Jack's mouth twisted. 'I'm not good for you. I'm hard
and cynical, frequently bitter. I have seen so many bad
things. You're arty and creative and...innocent. Un-
tainted.'

'No, I'm not.' Ellie pursed her lips. He made her sound
like a nun. 'You're not a bad man, Jack.'

'But I'd be bad for *you*.' Jack dropped his arms and
stared out to sea. 'I am not a noble man, Ellie, but I'm
trying to do the right thing here. Help me out, okay?'

Ellie lifted her hands in puzzlement. 'How am I supposed to do that?'

Jack glared at her. 'Well, for starters you could stop
looking at me as if you want to slurp me up through a
straw. Sexy little dresses like that don't help—and you're
very lucky that you kept possession of that thing you call
a bikini this afternoon. Short shorts and tight tops are
out too...'

'Would you like me to walk around in a tent?' Ellie
asked sarcastically, but secretly she was enjoying the fact
that she could turn him on so quickly. It was a power
she'd never experienced before, a heady sensation knowing that this delicious man thought that she was equally
tasty.

'That might work,' Jack replied.

Ellie pulled in a breath as he stepped forward and took

her much smaller hand in his. His expression turned sober.

'El, I like you, but I think you have enough going on in your life without the added pressure of an affair with me. I need to write your father's life story and I don't know how objective I'm going to be if I am sleeping with his daughter.'

Ellie kept her eyes on his and gestured him to continue. Everything he'd said so far had made sense, but she could still feel his lips on hers, his big hands on her skin. Taste him on her lips.

'It's been a long time since I just liked a woman, enjoyed her company. Can we keep this simple? Try to just be friends? That way, when I leave, there won't be any... stupid feelings between us.' Jack stared down at her fingers. 'You know it's the smart thing to do.'

Ellie sighed and wished she could be half as erudite as he was. Sure, words were the tools of his trade, but he made her feel as thick as a peanut butter sandwich when it came to expressing herself. Only two words came to mind, and neither were worthy of this conversation.

'Yeah, okay,' she muttered.

Jack smiled and ran his thumb over her knuckles before dropping her hand. 'So, will you go to the camping store for a tent or shall I?'

'Make sure it's a pink one.' Ellie looked around and her expression softened. 'Oh, we're here!'

'Where?' Jack asked as she grabbed the edge of his shirt and tugged him across the road.

Ellie walked up to some wrought-iron gates and

wrapped her fingers around the bars, looking at the dilapidated double-storey building.

Jack tugged on the chain that held the gates together. 'What *is* this place?'

'It was a library at the turn of the century, then it was turned into a house, but it's been empty a couple of years. I've heard a rumour that old Mrs Hutchinson is finally considering selling it. Restored, this building would be utter perfection. Two storeys of whimsy, with balconies and bay windows galore. Its irregular shape reminds me of a blowsy matron in a voluminous skirt and a peculiar hat. Romantic, eccentric and very over the top.'

Jack immediately picked up where she was going with this. 'You're thinking of this place for the bakery?'

'It's just around the corner from the present location, with ample parking space. I took a box of cupcakes to the Town Planning office and...well, bribed them into letting me take a look at the building plans. There is a lot of space, but not too much...enough to hold the bakery, the delicatessen and a proper breakfast and lunch restaurant.'

Jack put his hands on his hips. 'It's difficult to comment without seeing the place. Let's go in.'

Ellie pointed at the sign on the fence. '"No Trespassers".'

'If I obeyed those signs I'd never get a story,' Jack said, and pulled at a rusty iron post on the fence. It moved, and he gestured Ellie through the gap he'd created. 'You're slim enough to climb through here.'

'And you?'

Jack grabbed the top of the fence with his hands, yanked himself up and held his body weight while he swung his legs onto the railing. Within seconds he was on the other side and his breathing hadn't changed.

Ellie shook her head as she slipped through the fence. 'If you've split open your cut you're going to the emergency room,' she told him.

'Yes, Mum.' Jack grinned and led her up to the huge front door. He pursed his lips at the lock. 'No breaking in through *this* door.'

'We're not breaking in through any door!' Ellie stated as he pulled her away from the front door and around the house. 'Seriously, Jack, that's a crime!'

Jack peered through a window. 'Relax, there's nothing to steal, so if we get caught we can plead curiosity. I'm good at talking my way out of trouble.'

'Jack!'

Jack stopped at a side door. 'Good. Yale lock. Pass me a hairpin, El.'

'You are not going to... Hey!' Ellie slapped her hand against her head where Jack had yanked the pin from her hair. 'That hurt!'

'Sorry.' Jack opened the pin, inserted it into the lock and jiggled the handle. Within a minute the door swung open to his touch. 'Bingo.'

'I cannot believe that you picked that lock! Who taught you that?'

'You really don't want to know.'

Ellie looked curious. 'No, tell me. Who?'

'Your father, actually.'

Ellie rolled her eyes and Jack just grinned as he placed a hand on her lower back and pushed her inside.

'I *so* didn't need to know that!' she muttered.

'Relax.' Jack placed his hands on his hips and looked into the room to his right. 'Kitchen through here—an enormous one, but it needs to be gutted. God, Ellie, the ceiling is falling down!'

'I never said it didn't need work. Look at these floors, Jack. Solid yellow-wood.'

Jack looked at the patch of direct sunlight on the warped wood and at the hundreds of holes in it. 'White ants, Ellie, white ants. I bet the house is infested with them.'

'Are you always this pessimistic?' Ellie asked as she opened doors on either side of the passage.

'I just think you should slow down to a gallop. I can see the look in your eye. If you could you'd slap the deposit down,' Jack said. He picked at a piece of wallpaper and a strip came off in his hand. 'Before you even consider doing that I suggest you get an architect to look at the place, and a civil engineer to check that it's not going to fall down.'

It was sensible, unemotional advice—but sensible was for later. Right now she wanted to feel, sense, imagine.

Jack ducked his head into another room and Ellie heard what she swore was a screech. 'Did you squeal?' she called.

Jack hurried out of the room. 'Girls squeal. Men... don't. A rat nearly ran over my shoe! I hate rats!'

'Well, you squeal like a girl, and I'd rather have rats than white ants,' Ellie replied as they stepped into a massive hallway which was dominated by a two-storey-high ceiling and a thoroughly imposing staircase. Coloured sunshine from the stained glass inserts next to that imposing front door threw happy patterns onto the wooden floor.

'Okay, this is amazing,' Jack admitted.

'It's unbelievable,' Ellie said, falling hard.

Nothing had prepared her for the immediate visceral connection she felt to this property. She walked to the bay window behind the staircase and looked out onto the wilderness beyond, with its overgrown shrubs and trees. She could easily imagine the rambling, once stunning gardens that surrounded the house, like carefully chosen accessories on a red-carpet dress. Ellie walked the area downstairs and quickly established that the place could, without a huge amount of construction, be adapted to house the bakery.

It just took imagination—and she had lots of that.

'Why hasn't someone converted it into a restaurant? A bed and breakfast? An art gallery?' Jack asked when she rejoined him in the hall.

'Many have tried. Many have failed. Mrs Hutchinson hasn't ever been prepared to sell. She doesn't need the money and this building was her childhood home.' She shrugged at Jack's enquiring face. 'Basically, she's bats. The town fruitcake. She's refused offers—huge offers— for stupid reasons. Perceived lack of manners, not polishing your shoes. One man wore too much jewellery.'

'She sounds bonkers,' Jack said.

'That's one way of putting it,' Ellie said briskly, and tipped her head to look up at him. 'Let's finish with the breaking and entering. I could murder a drink.'

Jack followed her down the passage back to the side

door, which he yanked open for her. 'Technically, it was only entering. We didn't break anything.'

'Semantics,' Ellie said as he pulled the door shut behind him and they headed back down the winding driveway to the road.

'You really are a bit of a pansy, aren't you?' Jack leapt over the fence and jammed his hands in his pockets as he waited for her to climb back through the gate.

She was just straightening up when she heard a car approaching and slowing down. Ellie looked up and straight into the eyes of the driver, who was looking at her curiously.

'Oh, *dammit.*'

Jack looked from her to the disappearing Toyota. 'Problem?'

Ellie slapped the palm of her hand against her forehead. 'That was Mrs Khumalo, the busiest of St James's busybodies. Soon it will be all over town either that I am having secret trysts with a married man, or that I am buying the property, or that I'm joining a cult and this is going to be its headquarters.'

Jack laughed as she stomped down the road. 'Cool. As the great Oscar Wilde said, "There's only one thing in the world worse than being talked about, and that is *not* being talked about".'

'Grrr.'

They fell into an easy silence on their walk home from the pub, and Ellie enjoyed the fact that they could be quiet together, that neither of them felt the need to fill the space with empty words.

Jack took the keys from her hand and opened the front door for her, nudging the dogs out of the way with a gentle knee so that she could walk in first. In the hallway Ellie dropped her bag on the side table and placed her hands on her back, stretching while Jack examined the life-size nude painting of a blonde on a scarlet velvet couch on the opposite wall. She wore only her long hair and a waist-length string of pearls...and a very come-hither grin.

'I can't stop looking at this painting.'

Since it was a nude painting of a gorgeous woman, Ellie wasn't surprised. Most men had the same reaction.

'Who *is* that?'

'My best friend Merri.'

Jack stepped up to the portrait and lightly touched the canvas with the back of his knuckle. 'I meant the artist. The way he's captured the blue veins in her pale skin, her inner glow... God, he's amazing!'

Ellie felt a spurt of pure, unadulterated pleasure. 'Thanks.'

Jack's mouth fell open. '*You* painted this?'

'Mmm. I studied Fine Art at uni and lived in London for a while, but I couldn't support myself by selling my art so I came home and started work at the bakery.'

'It's brilliant. But you left out quite a bit between uni and coming back to Cape Town.' He touched the frame with his fingertips. 'And this is more than something you pass time with.'

Ellie felt the familiar stab, the longing to immerse herself in a big painting that sucked her into a different dimension. 'It used to be my passion. It isn't any more.'

'Why not?'

'I painted that just before I went to the UK. I'd finished uni and was going to conquer the world. I was so in love with art, painting, creating. I was...*infused* by art.'

Jack sat on the bottom stair and patted the space next to him. Ellie sat down and rested her arms on her knees, looking at Merri's naughty smile.

'Were you always arty?'

Ellie shrugged. 'I think I started when I was about six. I remember the first time I fell into a drawing.'

'Tell me.'

Ellie felt her voice catch. 'Mitchell was home. He'd just come back from somewhere in Africa. He was working in his study—nothing strange there—and the door was open. He was reading aloud an article he'd written...he did that. He read all his articles aloud.'

'He still does.'

'It was a report on the genocide happening in Rwanda—Burundi—somewhere like that. The report was graphic, horrific...' Ellie shuddered and felt Jack's strong arm around her waist, his hand on her hip. This time there was nothing sexual about his touch. It was pure comfort. 'Mitchell called it like he saw it: women, old people, children. Severed heads, limbs...'

'I know, sweetheart. Skip that part. Tell me about the art.' Jack rested his chin on her hair, shaken by the idea of a little girl hearing that. Damn Mitch and his stupidity. The man was a talented journalist, but as a father... useless.

'I couldn't get the pictures his words conjured out of my brain and the only thing I could think of to do was draw. Happy things—butterflies, princesses. I had nightmares for a while, and I'd wake up and hit my desk to paint or colour.' Ellie sighed. 'Mitchell could never censor himself. He had no conception of sensibility—that young kids didn't need to know that sixteen Afghan rebels had been executed and their decapitated heads paraded through the streets as a warning and that he'd witnessed it. It drove my mother mad that he couldn't keep his mouth shut in front of me.'

'But you had your art?'

'I did. He reported on brutality and war, violence, and I tried—still try—to counter that by producing beauty. It used to be through oils. Now it's through cake and icing.' Ellie shrugged and managed a smile.

Jack saw her staring at Merri's portrait and caught the pain and sadness in her eyes. There was more to this story or he wasn't a journalist. 'Why did you give it up?'

'Can we skip this part?' Ellie asked with a wobble in her voice.

'I'd really like to know.' Jack lowered his voice, made it persuasive.

'You ask me all these questions but you won't talk about yourself,' Ellie complained.

True. 'I know. I'm sorry. But tell me anyway.'

'Short story. He was the owner of an exclusive art gallery in Soho.' Grigson's, Jack remembered. The short blond from that photo in his room. 'He offered me an exhibition, told me I was the next big thing. I fell deeply, chronically in love with him. I found out later that was his *modus operandi.* I wasn't the first young artist he'd seduced into bed with that promise.'

Jack winced.

'I was swept away by him. He dealt in beauty and objects of art. He was a social butterfly—had invitations to something every night of the week. But he never took me along to anything. Like my father, he dropped in and out of my life. I kept asking him about the exhibition, spending time with me, taking me along, but he kept fobbing me off.'

'Bastard,' Jack growled.

'I told him that I wanted to break it off and he responded by proposing. I thought that meant that he'd change, but nothing did. I saw less of him than ever.'

'So what precipitated the break-up?' Jack briefly wondered why he was so interested in her past, why he felt the need to find the jerk and put him into a coma.

'I told him that I was done with waiting around for him. He responded by telling me that I was a mediocre artist who'd never amount to anything. That he'd just wanted to sleep with me occasionally but I wasn't worth the hassle...that it was, essentially, not worth my being around, him trying to keep me happy.'

Forget the coma. He now had the urge to put the guy six feet under. When Mitch had mentioned him he'd initially felt sorry for him, because he'd thought that she must have been pushing him into marriage, but he was the one who'd messed *her* around, messed her up. No wonder she tried so hard to be indispensable to the people she loved; she thought she had to try harder to be loved.

The two men she'd loved the most had hurt her, damaged her the most. God, the ways that love could mess

up people. Just another reason why he wanted nothing
to do with it...

'Anybody since then?' Jack asked, although he knew
there hadn't been.

'No.'

Needing to move, to work off his anger, Jack jumped
up and jogged up the stairs to inspect another painting.
He placed his hands on his hips and looked around at the
art covering the walls.

'Good grief, Ellie, some of these paintings are utterly
fantastic. I'm trying to work out which ones are yours,
because not all of them are.'

'Some are by fellow art students; others I've picked
up along the way,' Ellie said, pride streaking through her
voice. 'You like art?'

'I love art. Sculpture. Architecture,' Jack confirmed,
quickly moving up the stairs to examine a seascape.

He placed a hand on his hip and winced at the movement. Ellie watched his body tense. His face was illumi-
nated by the spotlight above his head. The violet shadows
beneath his eyes were back and his face was pale beneath
his slight tan.

Jack Chapman, she decided, had no concept of how to
pace himself. He'd recently suffered a horrendous beating, had a nasty knife wound, and yet he'd spent the day
sightseeing. She could see that he was exhausted and in
pain, and she knew that he was one of those men who
would carry on until he fell down.

He came across as easygoing and charming but there
was a solid streak beneath the charm, a strength of character that people probably never saw beneath the good

looks and air of success. His thought-processes were clear-headed and practical. While he'd challenged her decisions and her actions she didn't feel as if he was judging *her*.

He'd coaxed her past out of her and he was a fabulous listener. He listened intently and knew when to back away from the subject to give the guts-spiller some time to compose themselves.

Ellie caught his slight wince as he walked back down the stairs and she shook her head at him. 'For goodness' sake—will you sit down before you fall down?'

Jack's strong eyebrows pulled together. 'I'm fine.'

'Jack, you're not fine. You're exhausted and your body is protesting. Take a seat in the lounge, watch some TV. Do you want something to drink?'

Jack raked his hand through his hair. 'Nothing, thanks. Mind if I veg out on the veranda for a while?'

'Knock yourself out,' Ellie said. 'I'll plate up the Chinese.'

'Hey, El?' Jack called.

Ellie poked her head around the kitchen door. 'Yes?'

Jack rattled off an Arabic curse and Ellie wrinkled her nose. 'Something...something donkey. Sorry...what?'

'I just called your ex a bleeping-bleeping horse's bleeping ass.'

Ellie laughed. *Nice, Jack.*

After supper they headed back to the veranda and watched as dusk fell over the long coastline. Lights winked on as they sipped their red wine, sharing the couch with their bare feet up on the stone wall. Jack placed his arm along the back of the couch and Ellie felt his fingers in her hair. She turned to look at him but Jack was watching her hair slide between his fingers.

'It's so straight, so thick.'

Ellie felt his hands tug the band from her hair and felt the heavy drop as her hair cascaded down her back, could imagine it flowing over Jack's broad hand. She heard his swift intake of breath, felt his fingers combing her hair.

'I love the coloured streaks. They remind me of the flash of colour in a starling's wing.'

There was that creative flair again—this time with words. And there was that sexual buzz again. Ellie licked her lips. 'They're not my real hair.'

'Still pretty.' Jack lifted a strand of her hair and because it was so long easily brought it to his nose. 'Mmm... apple, lemon...flour.'

Ellie could not believe that she was so turned on by a man sniffing her hair. 'Jack...'

His eyes deepened, flooded with gold. He drifted the ends of her hair over his lips before dropping it and sliding his big hand around her neck. 'Yeah?'

Ellie dropped her eyes. 'We weren't going to do this, remember?'

'Shh, nothing is going to happen,' Jack said.

He dropped his arm behind her back, wrapped it around her waist and pulled her so that she was plastered against his hard body. Ellie swung around and rested her head against his chest, deeply conscious of his warm arm under her breasts.

'Did you submit your piece on that Somalian pirate-slash-warlord?' Ellie asked, to take her mind off the fact that she wanted to move his hands to more deserving areas of her body. Her breasts, the backs of her knees, between her legs.

'Yes. I didn't get as much information from him as I wanted to, but it was okay.'

'Have you worked out what you said that set him off?'

She felt Jack shake his head. 'Nah. I think he was high...and psychotic.'

'That might be it.' Ellie rested her hands on his arm, feeling the veins under his skin. 'Tell me about yourself. Mother? Father? Siblings?'

'Like you, I was an only child. I'm not sure why,' Jack replied.

Ellie half smiled. 'Tell me what you were like as a kid.'

She felt him stiffen at her question. 'At what age?'

Strange question. 'I don't know...ten?'

Jack's laugh rumbled through his chest. 'Hell on wheels. Maybe that's why my folks didn't have another kid. They probably despaired in case they'd have another boy.'

Ellie laughed. 'You couldn't have been *that* bad.'

'I was worse. Before I was eight I'd broken a leg, had three lots of stitches and lost most of my teeth.'

Ellie's mouth fell open. 'How on earth did you manage to do that?'

'The broken leg came from ramping with my BMX. The ramp I'd built myself collapsed. The teeth incident was from a fight with Juliet Grafton. I called her ugly—which she was. She was also built like a brick outhouse and her father was a boxing champion. Her mean right hook connected with my mouth. Stitches—where do I start? Falling off bikes, roofs, rocks...'

Ellie raised an eyebrow.

'But I was cute. That counted for a lot.'

She wanted to tell him he was still cute, but she suspected he already knew that, so instead she just watched night fall over the sea.

SIX

——

ELLIE WALKED INTO the ballroom on Jack's arm and looked around the packed space, filled with black-suited men and elegant women. His appearance caused a buzz and Ellie felt the tension in Jack's arm as people turned to watch their progress into the room. To them he was a celebrity, and well respected, and a smattering of applause broke out.

Jack half lifted his hand in acknowledgement. When he spoke, he pitched his voice so that only she could hear him. 'Those are the most ridiculous shoes, Ellie.'

Ellie grinned at the teasing note in his voice. He'd already told her that he liked her shimmery silver and pink froth of a cocktail dress, and she knew that her moon-high silver sandals made her calves look fantastic. She *felt* fantastic; she was sure it had a lot to do with the approval in Jack's expressive eyes.

'And, as I said, that is a sexy dress. Very you. Bright, colourful, playful.'

Ellie looked around and half winced. 'Most women are wearing basic black.'

'You're not a basic type of girl. And colour suits you.' He touched the hair she'd worked into a bohemian roll, with curls falling down her back. 'Gorgeous hair...make-me-crazy scent...'

'So I'll do?'

Jack took her hand and his words were rueful. 'Very much so.'

Ellie smiled with pleasure, then lifted her eyebrows as a tall blonde with an equine face stalked up to Jack, took his hand and kissed his cheek. Jack lifted his own eyebrows at her familiarity as she introduced herself as the Chairperson of the Press Club. Ellie forgot her name as soon as she said it.

'I have people who'd like to meet you,' she stated in a commanding voice.

'I'd like to get my date a drink first,' Jack said, untangling himself from her octopus grip.

'Ellie?'

Ellie turned at the deep voice and looked up into laughing green eyes in a very good-looking face. 'Luke? What are *you* doing here?'

'St Sylve is one of the club's sponsors,' he told Ellie, after kissing her on the cheek. He held out his hand to Jack. 'Luke Savage.'

'You drink Luke's wine all the time at home, Jack,' Ellie told him after they'd been introduced. 'Where's Jess, Luke?'

Luke looked around for his fiancée and shrugged. 'Probably charming someone for business.'

'Jack, I really *must* take you to meet some people.'

The blonde tugged on Jack's sleeve and Ellie caught the irritation that flickered in his eyes.

Jack looked at Ellie and then at Luke. 'Will you be okay?'

Ellie smiled at him. 'Sure. I'll hang with Luke and Jess and see you at dinner.'

Jack nodded and turned away.

Ellie looked up at Luke and pulled a face. 'We're going to be placed at some awfully boring table, I can tell, with Horse Lady neighing at Jack all night.'

Luke grinned. 'Well, we're sitting with Cale and Maddie—'

Ellie squealed with excitement. 'They're here too?'

'Cale *is* a sports presenter and journalist, El.'

'I *so* want to sit with you guys!' Ellie fluttered her eyelashes up at him.

Luke winked at her. 'We'll just have to see if we can make that happen.'

Ellie felt a feminine arm encircle her waist and turned to look into her friend's laughing deep brown eyes.

'Are you flirting with my husband-to-be, Ellie Evans?'

Ellie laughed and kissed Jess's cheek. ''Fraid so.'

'Can't blame you. I flirt with him all the time. Now, tell me—why and how are you here with the very yummy Jack Chapman?'

Luke had somehow organised that they were all at the same table, and Jack felt himself relaxing with Ellie's charming group of friends. They were warm and down-to-earth and Jack was enjoying himself.

He leaned closer to Ellie and lowered his voice. 'How do you know all these people?'

Ellie sent him a side-glance out of those fabulous eyes. 'Maddie and I went to uni together. I met Luke through her, and Cale—he and Cale are old schoolfriends. But I've known Jess for years and years—before she and Luke met. Her company does Pari's advertising.'

'So, El,' Luke said as he picked up a bottle of wine from the ice bucket on the table and topped up their glasses with a fruity Sauvignon, 'what's this I hear about you having to move your bakery?'

Ellie wiped her hands on a serviette and pulled a face. 'I have to find new premises in less than six months.'

'And have you found anything?' Cale asked.

'Maybe. There's an old building close to the bakery that might work. It's supposed to be on the market, but I need to find an architect—someone who can look at the house and tell me if it's solid and if I can do the alterations I'm thinking of—before I put in an offer.'

Luke looked at Cale and they both nodded. 'James.'

'Another friend from uni?' Jack asked with a smile on his face.

Luke and Cale laughed, but didn't disagree with him. Luke told Ellie that he'd send her his contact details and the rest of the table moved onto another subject.

'Are you seriously considering that building for the bakery?' Jack asked Ellie, resting his cheek on his fist.

'Maybe. Possibly.' Ellie fiddled with her serviette. 'I'll speak to James and see what he says. Then I'll have to run it by my mum.'

'Understandable, since Pari's will be paying for it.' Jack

saw something flash across her face and frowned. '*You're* paying for it? How would you...? Sorry—that has nothing to do with me.'

'How would I pay for it? It's fine. I don't mind you asking. Ginger—my grandmother—set up a trust for me when I was little and she's pretty wealthy. Pari's would pay me rent. That's if I actually decide to buy and renovate the building.'

There it was again—that lack of confidence in her eyes. 'Why do you doubt yourself?'

'It's a lot of money, Jack.' Ellie twisted the serviette through her fingers. 'What if it's a disaster? What if I end up disappointing my mother, Merri, my grandmother Pari's memory...? God, my *customers*?'

'That's a lot of disappointing, El. And a lot of what-ifs.' Jack placed his hand on hers and held them still. 'You love that building. Yours eyes light up when you talk about it. When are you going to start trusting yourself a little more?'

Ellie bit that sexy bottom lip—the one he wanted so badly to taste again.

'Merri says that I'm too much of a people-pleaser. That I have this insane need to make the world right for everyone.'

He didn't think Merri was wrong. 'You need to start listening to yourself more and to underestimate yourself less.'

Ellie twisted her lips. 'And not to think that I'm indispensable and the world will stop turning if I say no... I'm a basket case, Jack.'

Jack sent her an easy grin. 'We're all basket cases in

our own way. You're just a bit more...vulnerable. Softer than most.'

'I need to grow a bit more of a spine.'

'I think you're pretty much perfect just as you are.'

Jack sighed as the Master of Ceremonies started to talk. He'd much rather talk to Ellie than listen to boring speeches. He heard the MC introducing him and grimaced. His was probably going to be the most boring speech of all. He felt Ellie's hand grasp his knee and a bolt of sexual attraction fizzed straight through him.

'You didn't tell me that you were making a speech!' she hissed.

He stood up, buttoned his jacket and looked down at her. 'Yeah, well, for some reason they find me interesting.'

'Weird. I simply can't understand why,' Ellie teased.

Jack swallowed his laughter before moving away from her and heading for the podium, thinking that he could think of a couple of things he'd rather be doing than giving a speech. Top of the list was doing Ellie. In the pool, in the kitchen, in the shower...

Jack reached the podium, looked at the expectant faces and let his eyes drift over to his table. Luke raised his glass at him. Maddie rested her arms on the table and sent him a friendly smile. Ellie, being Ellie, pulled a quick tongue at him and he swallowed a grin.

There wasn't much wrong with the world if Ellie was in it, making him laugh.

It had been heaven to be in Jack's arms, even if it was just for a couple of slow dances around the edge of the dance floor. In her heels she'd been able to tuck her face into his neck, feel his warm breath in her hair, on her temple. There had been nothing demure about their dancing. They'd been up close and personal and neither of them had been able to hide their desire. Her nipples had dug into his chest and her stomach brushed his hard erection. Their breaths mingled, lips a hair's breadth apart. She was certain that someone would soon notice the smoke and call the fire brigade.

The music had changed now, from slow to fast, and Jack's broad hand on her lower back steered her back to their empty table. He pulled out a chair for her and looked from her to a hovering waiter.

'What can I get you to drink? G&T? A cocktail? Or do you feel like sharing a bottle of red wine?'

'That sounds good.'

Ellie crossed her legs as Jack took the chair next to her and flipped open the wine list he'd been handed. He held it so that Ellie could scan the selection with him.

Ellie tapped the list with her finger. 'I don't really care as long as it has alcohol and is wet. Any of Luke's wines are good. St Sylve's.'

She sounded nervous, Jack thought. So she should, even if she had only a vague idea of how close she'd come to being ravished on the dance floor.

Jack rubbed his forehead. *Ravished.* Only Ellie could make him think of such an old-fashioned word. Pulling himself together, he ordered the wine, then slipped off his suit jacket before loosening the collar on his white dress shirt and yanking down his tie in an effort to get more air into his lungs. Now, if only he could sort his tented pants out.

'That's better.'

Ellie touched her hair and smiled wryly. 'I wish I could do that to my hair.'

He wished *he* could do that to her hair. He'd spent many hours thinking about that hair brushing his stomach, about wrapping it around his hands as he settled himself over her... Jack shifted in his chair. What was *with* this woman and her ability to short-circuit his brain? He dropped his eyes to her chest, where the fabric of her dress flirted with her cleavage and showed just a hint of a lacy pink bra.

Kill me now, Jack thought.

Ellie draped a leg over a knee and looked across the room. He could see her rapidly beating pulse at the base of her neck and knew that she was just as hot for him as he was for her. Not that he needed any confirmation. The little brush of her stomach across his body on the dance floor had been a freaking big clue.

Their wine was delivered and their conversation dried up. Jack didn't care. He just wanted to drink her in, lap her up... He gulped his wine, thoroughly rattled at how sexy he found her. Deep blue eyes, that sensual mouth, the scent of her sweetly sexy perfume. She had such beautiful skin, every inch of which he wanted to explore, taste, caress...

Sitting there, looking at her, he became conscious of something settling inside of him... To hell with being sensible and playing it safe. He knew what he wanted and he was damn well going to ask for it.

He reached over and lightly rested the tips of his fingers on the inside of her wrist, smiling wryly when he felt her pulse skitter. He lifted his hand, pushed a strand of hair that had fallen over her eyes behind her ear.

He leaned over and spoke in her ear. 'I can't do this any more. I've tried everything I can to resist you but enough is enough. Let's go home. Let me take you to bed.'

He saw the answer in her eyes and didn't wait for her nod before taking her hand and leading her—wine, function and friends forgotten—out of the room.

Jack waited while she locked the front door and then backed her up against it, his body easily covering hers. He'd removed his jacket and she could feel the heat from his body beneath his shirt. His chest flattened her breasts and her breath hitched in response. This was so big, she thought, so overpowering...

His hands were large and competent, stroking her waist and skimming her ribcage in a sensual promise of what was to come. His hands skirted over her bottom and he lifted her up and into him, forcing her to wrap her legs around his waist. His hands held her thighs, steaming hot under the frothy skirt of her favourite dress. One heel dropped to the floor and it took a slight shake of her other foot for her remaining shoe to drop as well. Jack's mouth finally brushed hers and his tongue dipped into her mouth in a long, slow slide.

Jack walked with her to the stairs and at the first step allowed her to slip down him. He cradled her head in his hands and rested his forehead on hers.

'Upstairs?' he whispered, and Ellie felt the word and his breath drift over her face.

She nodded, ordered her legs to move and lightly ran

up the stairs. She turned into her darkened bedroom and realised that Jack was a second behind her. He yanked her to him and walked her backwards to her big double bed. She felt the mattress dip under her weight, and dip some more as she was pushed on her back and Jack crawled over her.

She felt one of the straps of her dress fall down a shoulder and Jack's lips on her smooth skin. He was everything she'd ever wanted, she thought: strong, sexy, amazingly adept at making heat and lust pool in her womb. She'd never felt so intimately invested in a kiss, an embrace... so desperate to have his mouth on her, his fingers on her, to touch him, explore him, know him.

This could mean something, Ellie thought. This could mean something...huge.

Jack sat back on his haunches and pulled her up, kissing her as his hands looked for the zip at the back of her dress. Cool air touched her fevered skin as his hands wandered and soothed, danced over her skin, while his tongue did an erotic tango with hers.

Then her dress fell to her waist and she half sat, half lay in her strapless bra, her torso open to his hot gaze.

It had been so long. She'd half forgotten what to do. Should she undo the buttons of his shirt, pull it over his head? Let him do it himself? Could she do that? Should she do that? Ellie brushed her hand over his hip and felt the padding of his dressing. Another thought dropped into her scrambled head. Should he even be doing this? What if he pulled the skin apart and he started bleeding again?

'Your cut...' Ellie murmured, sitting up in an effort to escape those searing eyes.

'Is fine,' Jack replied, stroking her from shoulder to hand.

Ellie rested her forehead on his collarbone and sighed. She wanted this, wanted to immerse herself in this experience with him, but suddenly her mind was jumping around like a cricket on speed, playing with thoughts that were not conducive to inspiring or maintaining passion. Thoughts like, What did this mean to him? To her? With all her previous lovers—okay, all two of them—she'd felt and given love and thought that that love was reciprocated to a degree. There was nothing like that with Jack. They had nothing more between them than a burgeoning friendship and a searing, burning passion.

It had been so long since Darryl, and she was so out of practice. Would she be enough for him? She had enough pride to want to get this right. Was she knowledgeable enough, sexy enough, passionate enough to make this something that he'd remember?

Jack pulled her dress over her head and ran his index finger above the edge of her bra, his finger tanned against her creamy skin. Ellie looked down at his finger and closed her eyes, confused and bemused. She wanted him, but she wasn't wholly convinced that she was ready...

She should say no. She needed to say no...

Jack looked down at her breasts spilling over her frothy bra and thought that he'd never seen anything as beautiful in his life. Her skin had a luminosity that he'd never seen before—the palest blush on a creamy rose. Her ribcage was narrow, her arms slim, and her fingers were still on his hip. He could feel the heat in them through his pants, as tangible as her very sudden, very obvious mental retreat.

Going, going...oh, crap...*gone*.

Jack knew that he could kiss her, could stoke those fires again, but if she wasn't as fully in the moment with this as he was—had been—then it wasn't fair to her or—*dammit*—to him. He wanted her engaged, body, mind and soul. He could have physical sex with other women. He wanted, *expected* more from Ellie. Why and how much more he wasn't sure, but still...

Jack ran his hand over her head and sat back, his knees on either side of her legs. Ellie looked at him with big, wide eyes the colour of blue moonlight and ran her tongue over her top lip. He really wished she wouldn't do that... it made him think of the plans he'd had for that tongue. Hot, wicked, sexy plans.

Dammit... He sighed.

There were a bunch of reasons why he shouldn't be doing this, he thought. All of them valid. He was here for a limited time and she wasn't the type of girl who indulged in brief affairs. They were already living in the same house, so if they slept together they'd step over from friendship into sex-coloured friendship which was the gateway for affection, which led to attachment and a myriad of complications.

And what if that happened and he found himself liking living with her and not wanting to leave? How could he reconcile that with the promise he'd made to himself and to others that he'd live life to its fullest? His hard, fast, take-no-prisoners lifestyle—a life spent on planes, trains and hotel rooms—was not conducive to a full-time lover and invariably led to disappointment and sometimes to disaster.

'Jack?'

Jack blinked and lifted his eyebrows. 'Mmm?'

'You're a bit...heavy,' Ellie said in a small voice.

Jack immediately moved off her legs and sat on the edge of the bed. 'Sorry,' he muttered.

'No, it's okay. Just...um...need to get my blood circulating,' Ellie said in a jerky voice.

Jack sat sideways on the bed and thought that Ellie looked breathtaking in the low light that spilled into the room from the passage. Her mouth was soft and inviting and her hair was mostly out of its elaborate style, falling in waves over her shoulders.

Jack, all concerns forgotten, started to lean forward, intent on kissing the life out of her, but he made the mistake of looking into her eyes. They were round and slightly scared—and utterly, comprehensively miserable. He wondered how long it would take for her to call it quits, how far she'd take him down the road before she realised that she wasn't mentally ready to sleep with him.

It turned out not to be long at all...

'I'm sorry.' Ellie's voice was jerky and full of remorse. 'I really can't do this.'

So, she did have guts. Good to know, Jack thought. And at least she was honest.

'Okay.'

Jack saw Ellie cross her arms over her chest so he stood up and walked over to her bedroom door, unhooked her dressing gown. He passed it to her and moved on to stand at her open window, looking out at the dark night. When he turned around again Ellie's gorgeous body was covered, chest to knee, in a silky wrap that was almost as heart-attack-inducing as the dress she'd worn earlier.

He had to get out of her room before he did something he would regret. Like haul her back into his arms.

So he walked over to her and dropped a kiss on her temple. 'It's late. Maybe we should get some sleep.'

He thought it was a tragedy when Ellie didn't try to stop him when he walked out of the room.

Ellie woke, dressed and stumbled down the stairs half asleep. The noise of the television from the lounge jerked her fully awake and immediately caused memories of the previous night to rush back with the power of a sumo wrestler. She groaned. Jeez, she'd had all the sophistication of a pot plant. It had been so long, and she'd been so nervous, so self-conscious and hadn't been able to stop the weird thoughts buzzing around her head. She'd been worried about him seeing her naked and she'd stressed about whether he would stay the night with her, how much foreplay he expected and whether he was enjoying himself.

She'd been unable to let go, and if she was so attracted to him shouldn't she be able to lose herself in him? Wasn't that what lust-filled lovers did?

Ellie stood in the doorway to the lounge and stared at her wooden floor.

'Morning,' Jack said from the corner of the room, where he sat in a violet chair, leaning forward, his hands loose between his knees.

Elle lifted her head and squinted at him. 'Morning. How long have you been up?'

'Not too long.'

Ellie rested her hand on the doorframe. 'I'll go and make coffee.'

Jack nodded to a steaming cup of coffee that stood on the coffee table. 'I heard you moving around as I came down the stairs so I made you a cup.'

'Thanks.' Ellie walked across the room to pick up her cup and wrapped her hands around it. The purple elephant was back and was laughing like a maniac. But she wasn't going to consider raising the subject. It was embarrassing enough thinking about it. Talking to him about it would be absolutely impossible!

And that was even before she realised how preoccupied and distant Jack looked.

'I thought I'd get caught up with what's happening in the world. Do you mind?' he said.

'No.'

He gestured to the TV. 'Your dad is in Kenya, reporting on the riots.'

Okay, she'd go with world politics if that was all he had. 'They are having elections soon,' he added.

She *so* didn't care. She wanted to know what he was going to do now, how she was supposed to act. Ellie bit her lip, walked further into the room and looked at her father's familiar face on the screen.

'He's looking tired.' Ellie sat down on the couch and tucked her legs up under her as Mitchell answered questions from the anchor in New York.

'He texted me earlier. He thinks there's big trouble brewing.'

Jack turned up the volume on the TV set and she listened with half an ear as Mitchell spoke about the situation in Kenya. *He's nearly sixty*, Ellie thought, wondering whether he had any thoughts about retiring. Because that wasn't something he'd ever discuss with *her*.

'I'm going there.'

Ellie took a moment to assimilate his statement. 'Going where?'

'To Kenya. A massive bomb was found and defused and the country is on a knife edge. I have contacts there,' Jack explained. He lifted his cup. 'I'm going to head out as soon as I've finished my coffee.'

'Ah...'

'I'm the closest reporter, and if I can get on a flight now I'll be with Mitch within a couple of hours. He's going to need help covering this.'

'Why?'

Jack frowned. 'It's news, Ellie, and news is my job. I know Nairobi. I want to be there.'

Ellie's heart sank. Of course he did. It didn't matter that he was beaten up, hurt and tired, or that he'd kissed her senseless, there was a story and he needed to follow it. It was the nature of the beast.

The fact that she was acting like a nervous, awkwardly shy Victorian nerd was also a very good excuse for him to run from her—fast and hard. Could she blame him?

Ellie refocused as Jack answered his ringing mobile. 'Hey, Andrew. No, I managed to get a seat on the next flight out to Nairobi. I'll be at the airport in—' he looked at his watch '—an hour. In the air in three.'

It took forty-five minutes to get to the airport, which left fifteen minutes for him to pack up and walk out of her life, Ellie thought. Last night she'd been lost in this man's arms and this morning he was making plans to walk out through the door without giving her a second thought.

And that just summed up all her experiences with war reporters. Nothing was more important than the story... ever.

Ever.

Jack leaned forward in his seat. He really didn't want to be on this plane, was unenthusiastic about going to Kenya, but all through the night, unable to sleep, he'd known that he couldn't stay with Ellie, that he needed to get some distance. From her...from the feelings she pulled to the surface.

Last night, for the first time in years, he'd allowed himself to become mentally engaged with a woman, and in doing so he'd caught a glimpse of all that he was missing by not allowing that intimate connection. The warmth of her smile, the richness of her laughter, her enjoyment of being with him all added another layer to the constant sexual buzz that took it from thrilling to frightening.

They'd been emotionally and physically in sync and he'd loved every second of the previous evening—even if she had called a halt to it. Hell, he'd loved every minute of the past few days. He could, if he let himself, imagine a lifetime of evenings drinking wine on the veranda, taking evening walks with her, making love to her.

Brent had never got to experience anything like this....

The thought chilled him to the bone. *Brent.* And, dear God, he needed to make a decision about going to that memorial service, to face his family...to face his demons, the never-ending guilt of being alive because that teenage boy was dead.

Jack rubbed his face. If he hadn't had a heart transplant, if he'd grown up normal, what would his life be like? Where would he be? What would he be? Would he be married yet? Have kids?

How much of his reluctance to get involved was his own reticent nature and how much was driven by guilt? Was he avoiding love and permanence not only because he felt that his job didn't allow it but also because he felt he didn't deserve it? That if Brent couldn't have it why should he?

He already had his heart—was he entitled to happiness with it as well? Jack let out a semi-audible groan.

The elderly lady next to him, with espresso eyes and cocoa skin, laid an elegant hand on his arm.

'Are you all right, my dear?'

Jack dredged up a smile. 'Fine, thanks.' He saw doubt cross her face and shrugged. 'Just trying to work through some stuff.'

She rattled off a phrase in an African language he didn't recognise.

'Sorry, I don't understand.'

'African proverb. Peace is costly but it is worth the expense.'

Indeed.

SEVEN

_____

ELLIE SNAPPED AT one of her staff and, after apologising, realised that she desperately needed a break from the bakery. Taking a bottle of water from the fridge, she walked out through the front door into the strong afternoon sunlight. Checking for cars, she walked across the street and sat on the concrete wall that separated the beach from the promenade and stretched out her bare legs. She flipped open the buttons of her chef's tunic and shrugged it off, allowing the sea breeze to flow over her bare shoulders in her sleeveless fuchsia top.

It had been four hellish days since Jack's abrupt departure. She had the concentration span of a flea and her thoughts were a galaxy away from her business and her craft.

His memory should have faded but she could still remember, in high definition, her time spent with Jack. The way his eyes crinkled when he smiled, the flash of white teeth, those wizard-like eyes that made you want to spill your soul.

She missed him—really missed him. Missed his manly

way of looking at a situation, his clear-headed thought-processes, and she missed bouncing ideas about Pari's off him. She missed her friend.

But more than missing him she was also now seriously irritated. Furious, in fact. Partly at Jack, for whirling out of her house like a dervish, but mostly at herself. How stupid was she to think that she could rely on him, that he wouldn't drop her like a hot brick for a story, for a situation?

The men she was attracted to always ran out on her, so why had she thought it would be different with Jack? He'd been in her life for under a week and she was livid that, subconsciously at least, she'd come to rely on him in such a short time. For advice, for a smile, for conversation and company at the end of a long day. How could she have forgotten, even for one minute, that war reporters always, *always* left, usually at a critical time in her life?

She couldn't help the memory rolling back—was powerless against the familiar resentment. She'd been fourteen and she'd entered a drawing of a lion into a competition in a well-known wildlife magazine. Out of thousands of entries throughout the country she'd won the 'Young Teenager' category. She'd been due to receive her prize at a prestigious televised awards ceremony. She'd spent weeks in a panic because Mitchell was on assignment, and the relief she'd felt when he'd arrived back home three days before the ceremony had been overwhelming.

Everything had been super-okay with her world. The thought of going up onto that stage in front of all those people had made her feel sick, but her handsome dad would be in the audience so she'd do it. She would move mountains for him.

Then someone had got assassinated and he'd flown out two hours before the event...which she'd been too distraught to attend.

Ellie straightened her shoulders. She was no longer that broken, defeated, sad teenager who'd flung her arms around her father and begged him not to go.

She sipped her water and narrowed her eyes. She'd looked up the political situation in Kenya, and while it was tense it wasn't exploding. Jack hadn't needed to hightail it out of her house. He was running from her—probably looking for an excuse to get away from her hot and cold behaviour, her lack of confidence in that sort of situation and her disastrous bedroom skills. If Jack had bailed just because of that, if she never saw him again—and who knew if she would, since *she hadn't heard from him since he'd left*—then good riddance, because then he was an idiot. As angry and...she searched for the word... *disappointed* as she felt, she knew that she was worth far more than just to be some transient woman who provided him a bed and some fun in it.

Ellie heard a long wolf whistle and looked up to see Merri leaving Pari's, two bottles of water in her hand. She'd obviously left Molly Blue with someone in the bakery—probably Mama Thandi—and was sauntering across the road as if she owned it.

Merri handed her another bottle of water and sat next to her, stretching her long body. A car passing them drifted as the driver gaped at her sensational-looking friend. Merri, as per normal, didn't notice. Ellie was quite certain that the majority of motor car accidents in Muizenberg were somehow related to Merri and the effect she had on men's driving.

'Now, tell me, why are you looking all grumpy and sorry for yourself?'

Ellie cracked open the second bottle of water and took a long swallow. How did she explain Jack to Merri?

The best way was just to blurt it all out. 'I nearly slept with Jack.'

'Good for you!' Merri gaped at her. 'Wait…did you say *nearly*? What is wrong with you, woman?'

There was no judgement in Merri's voice, and Ellie knew that her 'almost sleeping with Jack' story wouldn't even create a blip on her shock radar. Merri was pretty much unshockable.

Unlike her, Merri was a thoroughly modern woman. Not a drip.

'Do you want to talk about it?' Merri asked.

Ellie shook her head. 'Yes. No. Maybe. Still processing. Very confused.'

'So it wasn't just sex, then?'

'We didn't get that far. I said that I wasn't ready and he backed off.'

'Nicely?'

'What do you mean?'

'Was he nice about it? No tantrums, accusations, saying you led him on?'

Ellie shook her head. 'Of course not. He just passed me my dressing gown and said goodnight.'

'Huh. I *really* have to start dating nicer guys,' Merri

stated thoughtfully. 'So why couldn't you go through with it?'

Ellie looked out to sea and wondered if she could escape this conversation. As if sensing her thoughts, Merri hooked her arm in hers and kept her in place.

'It was fine—great. I was totally in the moment and then—' Ellie snapped her fingers '—like that, my brain started providing a running commentary.'

'Oh, I hate it when it does that,' Merri agreed. 'I remember being so caught up in the intensity of being with this one guy, and then he took off his shirt and he had a pelt of chest hair. And back hair. It was like he was wearing a coat...*ugh*. My brain started making jokes at his expense. Does Jack have back hair?'

'Uh...no.'

'Did he make animal sounds?'

'No.'

'Talk dirty?'

'No.'

'Have a really small—?'

'Merri!' Ellie interjected, cutting her off. 'He's fine—gorgeous, in fact! He didn't do anything wrong!'

'Then what was the problem?' Merri asked, puzzled. 'He's gorgeous, nice, and you were into him.' She looked Ellie in her eyes and twisted her lips. 'Ah, *dammit*, Ellie!'

'What?' Ellie demanded.

'When you told me that Jack was staying with you we talked about you getting emotionally entangled with him.' Merri shook her head in despair. 'And you have, haven't you?'

'I'm not entangled with him. Or at the very least I'm

trying not to get emotionally attached to him. When we were getting it on I had this thought that he could become a big thing if I let him.'

'And how is that *not* getting emotionally involved with him?' Merri demanded.

'The key phrase is *if I let him*,' Ellie protested.

Merri was silent for a while, and her voice was full of hope when she spoke again. 'Are you not just getting lust and feelings mixed up? Sometimes sex is just sex and it doesn't always have to be more.'

'I know that...and I tried to think that. Unfortunately I can't just think of him as a random slab of meat.'

'Try harder.' Merri sighed forlornly. 'Have I taught you nothing?' She narrowed her eyes in thought. 'Maybe you need to practise the concept of casual sex a bit more? I have a friend who is always up to...helping the cause.'

Ellie hiccupped a laugh at Merri's outrageous suggestion. 'Thanks, but no. Really.'

They both heard Merri's name being called, and across the street Mama Thandi stood with Molly in her arms, her face wet with tears. 'I'm coming!' Merri called back as she stood up.

She bent and kissed Ellie goodbye and a nearby jogger nearly ran straight into a lightpole.

Merri was right. She had to wrap her head around the concept of casual sex. And if—big if!—Jack came back, then she'd have to decide whether she could separate sex and emotion, because becoming emotionally attached to Jack would be a disaster of mega proportions.

They were fire and water, heaven and hell, victory and defeat. Maybe there *was* something fast and hot between them sexually, but fast and hot weren't enough to sustain a relationship. Relationships needed time and input, and at the very least for the participants within said relationship to be on the same continent for more than a nano-second.

Like Mitchell, Jack was the ultimate free spirit: an adventurer of heart and soul who needed his freedom as he needed air to breathe.

Apart from the fact that she didn't want to—was too damn scared to—become emotionally involved with a man who was just like her father, Ellie knew that she wasn't exciting enough, long term, for someone as charismatic as Jack. Darryl had put her childhood fears and suspicions into words five minutes before he'd left her life for good.

'You need to face facts, Ellie. You're not enough—not sexy enough, smart enough, interesting enough—for a man to make sacrifices for. Nobody will give up their freedom and time for monogamy with you. Nobody interesting, at least.'

It was something she'd suspected all her life, and having someone—him—verbalise it had actually been a relief. Even if it had hurt like hell.

Ellie watched the afternoon crowds walk down the promenade, smiling at the earnest joggers, the chattering groups of women walking off their extra pounds. Kids on bicycles weaved through the crowds and skateboarders followed in their wake. It was a typical scene for a hot day in the summer.

Ellie saw a taxi pull up across the road just down the street from the bakery before she half turned to look at the sea. A number of cargo ships hovered on the horizon and a sailboat zipped by closer to shore. Reaching for her bottle of water, she looked back at the bakery and saw a man climb out of the taxi, his hand briefly touching his side. His broad shoulders and long legs reminded her of Jack...but this man had short hair, wore smart chinos, a long-sleeved white shirt with the cuffs rolled back and dark, sleek sunglasses. Then the sun picked up the reddish glints in his hair...

Jack?

Ellie yelped and dropped her water bottle as he paid the driver and pulled that familiar black rucksack from the boot of the taxi.

Jack... Jack was back.

Oh, good God... Jack. Was. Back.

As if he sensed her eyes on him Jack straightened and looked across the road. Ellie folded her arms and bit her lip. There was no way that she was going to run across the road like a demented schoolgirl and hurl herself into his arms...as much as she wanted to.

Ellie gnawed on her bottom lip as he lifted his rucksack with one hand, dropped it over his shoulder and slowly walked across the road. When he reached her he dropped the rucksack at her feet and sent her a small grin.

'Hi, El.'

Ellie's stomach plummeted and twisted as her name rolled off his tongue. She tucked her hands into the back pockets of her jeans and rocked on her heels.

'You're back. And you cut your hair...' Ellie stuttered and her heart copied her voice.

The corner of Jack's mouth lifted as he brushed his hand over his short back and sides. 'Seems like it.'

'I thought you would've headed home...' Ellie said, wishing she could hug him and also that she could finish a sentence. What *was* it about this man who had her words freezing on her tongue?

His eyes didn't leave hers. 'I have a flat in London but it certainly isn't home.' His mouth lifted in that teasing way that she'd missed so much. 'Besides, I paid you for three weeks' board and lodging and I'd like to get my money's worth.'

Ellie grinned. 'That sounds fair.' She could smell him from where she stood: sandalwood and citrus, clean soap and sexy male. Ellie breathed him in and again wished she were in his arms.

She looked up into his face and sighed at the stress in his eyes, the deeper brackets around his mouth. 'Rough trip?'

He shrugged. 'I've had worse.' He took her hand and raised her knuckles to place a gentle kiss on them. 'I'm sorry I didn't call...I wasn't sure what to say.'

Ellie's eyes narrowed as she remembered that she was supposed to be cross with him. 'I have to say that when it's required you can vacate a house at speed.'

Jack pushed his hair off his forehead. 'Yeah, sorry. I'm not used to explaining my actions... I've been on my own for too long and I'm not good at stopping to play nice.'

Ellie pulled her hand out of his and tapped her finger against her chin. 'How's my dad?'

'He's fine.' Jack went on to explain what he'd done in Kenya, the outcome of the contact he'd made with his numerous sources. His words were brief and succinct but Ellie could hear the tension in his voice, saw pain flicker in and out of his eyes and wondered what he wasn't telling her.

'Something else happened. Something that rocked you.'

Shock rippled across Jack's face. Then those shutters fell over his eyes and he dropped his gaze from hers, looking down at the pavement. When he lifted his head again his expression was rueful. 'The sun is shining; it's a stunning afternoon. I want to go home, climb into my board shorts and hit the surf. I just want to forget about work for a while.'

Ellie wished she could join him but gestured to the bakery. 'I still have a couple of hours' work to do.'

'Of course you do. I'll meet you back here at closing time.' Jack picked up his rucksack and slung it over one shoulder. 'It's good to be back, El.'

Ellie watched him cross the street and turn the corner for home. Jack was back and the world suddenly seemed brighter and lighter and shinier.

That couldn't, in *any* galaxy, be good.

'So, he hasn't made a move on you again?'

'No, not even close. Then again, he's barely spoken to me,' Ellie answered Merri, who was in for the afternoon, helping her make Sacher Torte for an order to be picked up that evening.

Princess Molly Blue, as beautiful as her mother, was fast asleep on Mama Thandi's back, held in place by a light cotton shawl wrapped around her back and Mama's chest. Ellie looked at Mama, who was quickly plaiting strips of dough for braided bread; it really was a very efficient way to carry on working and let your baby be close to you. Ellie hoped Merri was taking notes.

'What do you mean?'

'He's been back for two days and I've barely seen him.' Ellie shrugged. 'We eat supper together and then he disappears to his room to work.' She tightened the ties of her apron and frowned. 'There are friends, lovers and acquaintances. Jack left as a friend, was briefly—sort of—a lover, and he's come back as the last.'

Merri split a vanilla pod and scraped out its insides with a knife. 'What changed? Do you think it was because you said no?'

Ellie separated the whites and yolks of eggs as she considered the question. 'I don't know. Maybe.'

'If that's the reason then he's a jerk of magnificent proportions,' Merri stated, adding the vanilla to butter and sugar and switching on the beater.

'He might as well be a guest in my B&B, except that he packs the dishwasher, makes dinner if I'm working late and even, very kindly, did a load of my laundry with his own. I just want my friend back,' Ellie added.

'No, you don't. You want to sleep with him,' Merri said in a cheerful voice.

'No! Well, yes. But I can't. Won't.'

'Uh...why?'

'Because, as you said, I can't seem to separate the emotion and the deed,' Ellie admitted reluctantly. 'If I sleep with him I risk—'

'Caring for him, falling in love with him. Why would that be the worst thing that could happen to you?'

Ellie viciously tipped the egg whites into another mixing bowl and reached for a hand-beater. 'I don't want to talk about this any more.'

'Tough.'

Ellie shut off the hand-beater and checked on the chocolate that was melting in a *bain-marie*. 'We don't have enough time for me to list the reasons...'

'Yes, we do. Spill.'

'He has a job I hate. He's never around. I don't have time for a relationship—'

Merri pointed a wooden spoon at her. 'Quit lying to yourself, El. The biggest reason you are so scared is because he doesn't need you, and we all know that you live to be needed.'

Ellie looked at her, shocked. 'That's so unfair.'

'Ellie, you take pride in being indispensable. You *need* people to need you. You need to love more than you need love, and you recognise that Jack doesn't need your love to survive, to function. You're terrified of being rejected...'

'Aren't we all?' Ellie demanded.

'No. Some of us realise that you can't force someone to love you just because you want him to.'

'Bully for you,' Ellie muttered mutinously.

Merri stared at her, her eyes uncharacteristically sombre. 'I don't think I ever realised until this moment how much your father's lack of attention and Darryl's scumbag antics scarred you.'

Ellie wanted to protest that she wasn't scarred, that she was just being careful, but she knew it wasn't true. She'd suspected for a long time that she was emotionally damaged, and Merri's words just confirmed what she'd always thought.

So maybe it was better that she and Jack kept their distance, kept the status quo.

'Can we talk about something else? Molly Blue? Is she teething yet?'

Merri grinned at her. 'No, I don't want to talk about my baby.'

She'd been talking about Molly for six months straight and she didn't want to talk about her now? How unfair, Ellie thought.

'I still want to talk about you. Let's talk about your inability to say no...'

Ellie, past the point of patience, threw an egg at her.

Ellie rolled over and looked, wide-eyed, at the luminous hands of her bedside clock. It was twelve-seventeen and she wasn't even close to sleep. Throwing off her sheet, she cocked her head as she heard footsteps going down the stairs.

It seemed she wasn't the only person who was awake.

Ellie pulled a thigh-length T-shirt over her skimpy tank. It skimmed the hem of her sleeping shorts. Deciding against shoes, she flipped her thick plait over her shoulder, left the room and walked down the darkened stairs. She knew where he'd be: standing on the front veranda, looking out to the moonlit sea.

He wasn't. He was sitting on one of the chairs, dressed in running shorts and pulling on his trainers. Ellie hesitated at the front door and took a moment to watch him, looking hard and tough, as he quickly tied the laces in his shoes. It was after midnight—why was he going for a run? It made no sense...

'What are you doing?' she asked, stepping through the open door.

Jack snapped his head up to look at her and she caught the tension in his eyes. 'Can't sleep.'

'So you're going for a run?'

Jack shrugged. 'It's better than lying awake looking at the ceiling.'

Ellie folded her arms and looked at the top of his head. For the past four days he'd been quiet, and tonight at dinner he'd said little, after which he'd excused himself as usual to do some work. Despite hoping that he'd come back downstairs, she hadn't seen him since he'd left the table.

Jack stood up and started to stretch, and Ellie wondered if this was Jack's way of expelling stress and tension. She might indulge in a good crying jag but he went running. Maybe, just maybe, she could get him to try talking for a change.

She crossed her arms as she stepped outside, then walked up to him and nudged him with her shoulder.

'Why don't you talk to me instead of hitting the streets?'

'Uh—'

'C'mon.' Ellie boosted herself up on the stone wall so that she faced Jack, her back to the sea. 'What's going on, Jack? Has something happened?'

Jack placed his arm behind his head to stretch out his arms and Ellie noticed his chest muscles rippling, his six-pack contracting, that nasty scar lifting. She forced herself to take her mind off his body and concentrate on his words.

'Nothing's happened...'

Dammit, he simply wasn't going to open up. Ellie felt a spurt of hurt and disappointment and hopped off the wall. 'Okay, Jack, don't talk to me. But don't treat me like an idiot by telling me that nothing happened!'

Ellie headed for the front door and was stopped by Jack's strong arm around her stomach.

'Geez, Ellie. Cool your jets, would you?'

Ellie whirled around, put her hands on his chest and shoved. Her efforts had no impact on him at all. 'Dammit, I just want you to talk to me!'

'If you gave me two seconds to finish my sentence then you'd realise that I am trying to talk to you!' Jack dropped his arms and pointed to the Morris chair. 'Sit.'

Ellie sat and pulled her feet up to tuck them under her, her expression mutinous. She'd give him one more chance, but if he tried to fob her off with 'nothing happened' again she'd shove him off the wall.

Jack sat on the edge of the wall. 'Kenya was a fairly routine trip in that nothing *unusual* happened. I hit the streets, found my contacts, got some intel, reported. I worked, hung out with the rest of the press corps.'

Ellie pulled a face. 'Sorry.'

Jack placed his hand behind his ear. 'What was that?'

Ellie glared at him. 'You heard me. So if the trip was fairly routine, then what's bugging you?'

'Exactly that...the fact that the trip felt so routine. Unexciting, flat.'

Ellie scratched her forehead. 'I'm sorry, I don't understand.'

'I'm not sure if I understand either. There are certain

reasons I do what I do. Why I do it. I need the adrenalin. I need to feel like I'm living life at full throttle.' Jack must have seen the question on her face because he shook his head. 'Maybe some day I'll tell you why but not now. Not tonight.'

Not ready yet. She could respect that. 'Okay, so you need the thrill, the buzz of danger...'

'Not necessarily danger—okay, I like the danger factor too—but in places or situations like that there's always a buzz, an energy that is so tangible you can almost reach out and taste it. I feed on that energy.'

'And there wasn't any this time?'

Jack closed his eyes. 'Oh, there was—apparently. Everyone I spoke to said that there was something in the air, a sense that the place was on a knife edge, that violence was a hair's breadth away. The journalists were buzzing on the atmosphere and I didn't pick up a damn thing. I couldn't feel it. I felt like I was just going through the motions.'

'Oh.'

'There are different types of war correspondent. There are the idealists—the ones who want to make a difference. There are the ones who, sadly, feed off the violence, the brutality. There are others who use it to hide from life.' Jack scrubbed his hands over his face. 'I report. Fullstop. Right from the beginning I knew that it wasn't my job to save the world. That my job was to relay the facts, not to get involved with the emotion. I have always been super-objective. I don't particularly like making judgement calls, mostly because I can always see both sides of the story. Nobody is ever one hundred per cent right.

But I always—*always!*—have been the first to pick up the mood on the street, the energy in the air.'

'Do you ever take a stand? Get off the fence?' Ellie asked him after a short silence. 'Make a judgement call?'

Jack thought about her question for a moment. 'Personally or professionally?'

'Either. Both.'

'When it comes to political ideologies I am for neutrality. Personally, I've experienced some stuff...gone through a lot...so when bad things happen I measure it up against what I went through and frequently realise that it's not worth getting upset about. So I don't get worked up easily, and because of that I probably don't get involved on either side of anything either.'

Whoa! Super-complicated man. 'Okay, so getting back to Kenya...'

'I made an offhand comment to Mitch about feeling like this and that led to a discussion about me. He said that I've become too distant, too unemotional, too hard. He used the word "robotic". *Am* I robotic, El?'

Ellie stood up, sat on the wall next to him and dropped her head onto his shoulder. 'I don't think you are, but to be fair I haven't seen you in that situation or seen you report for a long time—six months at least.'

'He also said that I'm desensitised to violence, that I don't see other people's pain. That I'm becoming heartless.'

That was rich, coming from her father, Ellie thought, the King of Self-Involvement. Except her father was very good at what he did, so he might have a point. But Ellie didn't believe that Jack was as callous as he or her father made him out to be. It was more likely that he used his emotional distance as a shield.

'Is not caring just a way to protect yourself from everything bad you've seen?'

Jack shrugged. 'I have no idea. Mitch said that I'm burnt out, that it's affecting my reporting, that I'm coming across as hard. He said that I need to get my head in the game, take some time off to fill the well. We had a rip roaring argument...'

'He sent you home?'

Jack looked rebellious. 'As much as he likes to think he does, Mitchell doesn't *send* me anywhere. I left because there wasn't much more to report on except for rehashing the same story.' Jack stared at his feet.

'Is he right? *Are* you burnt out?' Ellie asked quietly, keeping her temple on his shoulder.

'I don't know.'

'I think you need to give yourself a break. You were beaten up in Somalia, stabbed, kicked out of the country. You've just come back from a less than cheerful city. When did you last take a proper holiday, relax...counter all the gruesome stuff you've witnessed with happy stuff?'

'Happy stuff?'

'Lying on a beach, surfing, drinking wine in the afternoon sun. Napping. Reading a book for pleasure and not for research. Um...sleeping late. In other words, a holiday?'

'Not for a while. Not for a very long time,' Jack admitted, placing his broad hand on her knee.

'Thought so. Maybe you should actually do that?'

'I don't know how to relax, to take it easy. It's not in my nature. I like moving, working, exploring. I need to keep moving to feel alive.'

'Maybe that's what you've conditioned yourself to feel...but it's not healthy.' Ellie yawned and reluctantly lifted her head off his arm.

Jack stood up and ran a gentle hand over her hair. 'Get some sleep, El. There's no point in us both being exhausted.'

Ellie didn't think about it. She just stood up, wrapped her arms around his waist and laid her cheek on his bare chest. 'Don't beat yourself up, Jack. Mitchell might think he's always right, but he's not.'

'I kind of think he might be this time.'

'Well, I hope you didn't tell him that. You'll never hear the end of it.' Ellie placed her forehead on his chest and kept one hand on his waist.

Jack stood ramrod-straight and for the longest minute Ellie held her breath, certain that he would push her away. Eventually his arms locked around her back and he buried his face in her hair. Ellie rubbed her hands over his back, met his miserable eyes and ran her hand across his forehead, down his cheek to his chest. Her hands dropped, brushed the waistband of his shorts, and she felt tension—suddenly sexual—skitter through his body. She moved her hands to put them on his hips and felt his swift intake of air.

'I missed you,' he said, his voice gruff.

'I missed you too.'

Jack closed his eyes and his arms tightened and his lower body jumped in reaction to her words. She could feel his heat and response through her light cotton shirt and sleeping shorts and she wanted him...

She didn't want to want him. She couldn't afford to want him.

She forced herself to say the words. 'I need to go to bed, Jack.'

Jack immediately released her and she suddenly felt colder without his heat.

'Go on up. I'm going for a run.'

Ellie nodded. 'Thanks, by the way.'

One eyebrow rose. 'For...?'

'Talking to me. I thought you were mad at me, so it was a bit of a relief. Sorry I jumped to the wrong conclusion in the beginning.'

Jack sent her a small grin. 'Next time you jump to conclusions I won't give you a second chance.'

Ellie patted his chest. 'Yes, you will.'

'I'm afraid you're probably right,' Jack said softly, and jogged down the stairs.

The night was warm and the streets were deserted, and the sea was his only companion as he ran along the promenade, his feet slapping against the pavement. Sweat ran down his temples and down his spine into the waistband of his shorts. His body felt fluid but his mind was a mess.

God, it felt good to run. Apart from the fact that it kept his heart working properly, it was easier to think when he was running.

He hadn't lied to Ellie—he *hadn't* connected with the story or the atmosphere in Kenya and that worried him— but he certainly hadn't told her the whole truth. How could he? How could he explain to her that he'd spent his days in Kenya missing her, thinking about her? He'd never allowed anyone to distract him from the job at hand, yet she had. He'd be walking the streets, seeing an old man whittling away at a piece of wood, and he'd think Ellie would crouch down next to him and demand to know what he was creating. He'd drink his morning coffee at the hotel and wish he was standing on her veranda, watching the endless blues and greens of the sea.

His nights were a combination of fantasy and frustration, thinking about what he wanted to do to and with her amazing body.

When he'd seen her on the wall that afternoon he'd come back his thumping heart had settled, sighed. And he'd known he had the potential to fall deeper and deeper in trouble. Emotional trouble.

He'd known her for only days and she'd stirred up all these weird feelings inside him. Why? What was it about her that made him feel as if he'd stepped outside of himself? He could talk to her. He wanted to talk to her. Take this evening, for example. He would never have spoken to any of his previous girlfriends like that...hell, he'd barely *spoken* to them. He'd just flown in from wherever, climbed into bed, kept said girlfriend in bed until he needed to leave and then left. He didn't know how to act as part of a couple on an on-going basis, and before he'd landed in Cape Town he'd never come close to being tied down by anyone or anything. He excelled in saying goodbye and never looking back. He'd had a second chance at life and he'd made a promise to live it hard, because he'd always believed it would be an injustice to live a small life...to confine himself to a humdrum job...to be shackled by a house or a lover.

His beliefs, so firmly held for so long, were starting to waver.

And that was why he'd scuttled out of Ellie's house last week. He hadn't needed to go to Kenya but it had been a damn good excuse to put some distance between them.

Jack stopped and, breathing heavily, placed his hands on his hips. In the low light of the sodium streetlights he stared out to the breaking waves as clouds scuttled across the moon. Little in life made sense any more... He could easily have gone back to London after Kenya but he'd headed south instead. What was happening to him?

He'd been shot, beaten up and stabbed. He'd sneaked behind enemy lines, walked into the compounds of drug cartels, through whorehouses filled with the dregs of humanity who'd slit his throat just for the fun of it—just to get a story. He'd seen the worst of what people could do to each other and yet he'd never felt fear like this before...

He was terrified he was becoming emotionally involved with her—would do practically anything to stop that happening. Ellie had hit the nail squarely in one of their many conversations; he was an observer, not a participator. Involvement with her would require a decision, taking a stand for her, sticking around, partaking in a life together.

He didn't want to do that—wasn't ready to do that. Wouldn't do that. He needed to find some perspective, reconnect with his beliefs, reaffirm his values. Jack nodded at the sea. He had to make sure that he kept some emotional distance, guarded against any deepening of their relationship. It was the sensible decision—hell, it was the only decision.

And while he was making major decisions he really needed to decide what he was going to do about Brent's memorial service. Go or not? He was starting to feel that he needed to, that he needed to honour Brent, to say thank you for the gift of his life. But would seeing him make the Sandersons' day worse? Would being there deepen the guilt he felt?

Maybe he shouldn't go.

Jack swore as he resumed running. This was why it was better not to examine his thoughts and emotions too closely. It just confused him. And, talking about being confused, what had Ellie meant when she'd said she had thought that he was angry with her? Why would she think that?

Jack intended to find out.

EIGHT

———

JACK POUNDED UP the steps and flung open her bedroom door. He knew she wouldn't be asleep and she wasn't. She was sitting up in bed, working on her computer. Didn't she ever give work a rest?

'Why are you working?' he demanded crossly.

'I'm not. I'm catching up with friends.'

'At one in the morning?'

'Excuse me, at least *I'm* not the one running after midnight!' Ellie closed the lid of her computer and tapped her finger against it. 'Did you just burst in here to give me a hard time generally or was there a specific reason?'

Jack walked into the room and stood at the end of her bed. 'You said that you thought I was mad at you. Why, Ellie?'

Ellie plucked the sheet with her fingers and felt her face flaming in the dim light of her lamp. 'It's not important.'

Jack sat on the edge of the bed and placed his hand on her knee. 'I think it might be. Talk to me, El.'

Ellie shook her head and placed her computer on her

bedside table. 'Jack, it really doesn't matter since you haven't made any...since we're not...'

'Sleeping together?' Jack sounded puzzled. 'Are you upset that I'm *not* sleeping with you?'

'Yes...no. I don't know. I thought you'd changed your mind about...me.'

Jack's expression was pure confusion. 'Let me try and decode that from girl-speak. Firstly, I couldn't run out of your house, not call you, then come back and expect to jump into bed with you. I thought we needed some time, and I've been dealing with all this other crap, so...' Jack rubbed the back of his neck. 'I changed my mind...? Hold on a sec—did you think that I didn't want to sleep with you? Why on earth wouldn't I want to sleep with you?'

'Good grief, Jack, you can't expect me to verbalise it!' Ellie cried.

'Well, if you want me to understand what's going on in that crazy head of yours, *yes*! Because I am lost!'

'I wasn't any good and it couldn't have been much fun for you,' Ellie mumbled. 'And I backed off midway.'

There was a long silence and Ellie felt Jack staring at her head. When he eventually spoke Ellie could hear the regret in his voice.

'Have you been worried about that since I left?'

'Mmm.'

Jack swore. 'And I left here with a rocket on my tail, not even thinking... Dammit!'

Ellie looked up at him. 'So you weren't mad that I said no?'

'Disappointed? Yes. Cross? Absolutely not.'

'Oh.'

Jack played with her fingers. 'Why *did* you stop, by the way? What happened?'

'My brain started a running commentary as soon as we got to my bedroom. I started to second-guess what we were doing—what I was doing. And whether I was getting it right.'

Jack cradled her cheek with his hand. 'Making love is not a test to be graded, sweetheart. Come on—cough it up. What else were you worrying about?'

'Whether I was enough for you. Whether I was practiced enough. Cellulite...other crazy girl stuff.' Ellie stared at a point beyond his shoulder.

'You don't have a centimetre of cellulite, and if you do I *so* don't care. And if we're trading thoughts about that night then I should tell you that I'm sorry if I went too fast for you. I'd thought about having you so many times, in so many ways...and I guess I was nervous too.'

'Why were you nervous? You've had lots of sex before.'

'Yes, but I've never had sex with *you*!' Jack exclaimed. 'What? I'm not allowed to be nervous? I finally get the girl I've been fantasising about in bed and suddenly I'm a stud? It doesn't work like that, Ellie. The first time you make love to someone it's *always* the first time. I'm also worried about pleasing you. It never works out perfectly. We don't know each other's bodies, what the other person likes and/or doesn't like. It falls into place with time.'

Ellie continued to stare at her bedclothes.

'Sweetheart, I really need you to talk to me, to tell me what you're thinking,' Jack said quietly, his voice persuasive.

Ellie lifted her head and looked at him with sad eyes.

'Thank you for that—for saying all of that. And you're probably right. We just need time.'

'Exactly.'

Ellie held his gaze. 'But we have a problem. By my calculations, and from everything you've told me, you're staying another week at the most. Then you'll leave... probably around about the time we can start making mountains move. So my two questions are: how fair would that be to either of us? And, really, what would be the point?'

'It doesn't have to be love, Ellie. It doesn't have to be for ever. It can just be two people who are attracted to each other giving each other pleasure and company. The point can be...' Jack encircled her neck with his hand and smoothed his thumb over the tendons in her neck '...this.'

He touched the corner of her mouth with his.

'So sweet. Spicy.' He stroked her jaw and placed his lips on the spot between her jaw and her ear. 'Soft. The point can be that I think you have the most beautiful skin.'

Jack moved and dropped his other hand onto her bottom. In a movement that was as smooth as it was sexy, he pulled her onto his lap so that she straddled his thighs.

As sparks bolted down her inner thighs Ellie dimly remembered that she had to be pressing on his knife wound and tried to scramble off him. Jack's hand on her thighs kept her firmly in place.

'Nuh-uh—where are you going? I like you here,' he said.

'Your cut,' Ellie protested, her head dropping so that their noses were practically touching.

'I'm fine and you feel great,' Jack informed her, lifting

his head to nibble on her mouth. 'I love your mouth...' he murmured. 'Love your eyes...fantastic skin...'

He lifted his hands from her thighs and placed them on her chest, holding the weight of her breasts in his hands. Ellie moaned as he thumbed her nipples into gloriously sensitive peaks.

'As for these...these are simply a point of their own.'

Ellie couldn't find any words, was drenched in the wet heat of his voice. She arched her back and rolled her neck as she pushed into his hands seeking more.

'You are so beautiful...' Jack dropped his hands down to her waist.

She shook her hair out and it spilled down her chest, over her brief tank top. Jack leaned back and just looked at her, his caress as bold as his eyes.

'Take it off,' he said, his voice hoarse. 'Let me look at you.'

Somewhere in some place deep inside her Ellie knew that she should probably say no, that she should climb off his lap and be sensible, but instead she arched her back, pulled her shirt over her head and held the garment in place against her chest. She hadn't thought it was possible for Jack's eyes to darken with passion, but they did and she saw his jaw clench.

She felt feminine and powerful and wondrously, wickedly wanton.

'You're killing me here, woman,' Jack growled and he lifted his hand to yank the shirt away. His nostrils flared as he took in her creamy skin now flushed with arousal. He held her face in his hands. 'Trust me, El. I'm going to show you exactly what the point of this is...'

* * *

Ellie walked into the bedroom from the bathroom, wrapped in a towel from waist to mid-thigh and towel-drying her hair. She looked from the clock to Jack, who was lying crossways across the bed, spread out on his stomach. 'We've wasted a good portion of the morning.'

'Hush your mouth, wench. A morning in bed is never wasted,' Jack said as he stood up and stretched. He was totally self-confident about his body and he had a right to be, Ellie thought. Apart from the nasty scar on his chest, he was perfect.

'How did you get that scar?' Ellie asked.

Jack lifted his hand up to his chest and immediately turned away. 'Operation.'

Ellie rubbed the ends of her hair between the folds of the towel. 'What operation?'

Jack walked past her and swatted her backside. 'The one I had in hospital.'

He stepped into the *en-suite* bathroom and Ellie heard water hitting the shower door. Well, that had gone well. *Not*. Obviously his scar-causing operation was not up for discussion. Ellie wondered why not. It couldn't be that big a deal, surely?

Jack raised his voice. 'This is such a waste of water... you should've let me shower with you.'

Ellie smiled at herself in the dressing table mirror. 'I couldn't trust you not to have your wicked way with me again.'

She'd thought about yanking him into the shower with her but she didn't think she could stand another bout of that sweet, sweet torture. Or maybe she could—in an hour or two, when all her nerve-endings had subsided slightly.

'You like my wicked ways.' Jack's voice was chock-full of self-satisfaction.

'I do? How can you tell?'

'Well, I think your begging was a huge hint,' Jack said dryly, before she heard the shower door open and close.

Ellie pulled fresh underwear out of her dresser drawer and quickly slipped into a matching aqua-green set. White shorts and a pretty floral top were perfect for a day to be spent at home...she had to stock up on cleaning products and dog food, spend some time on the internet paying personal bills, and she needed to finalise the arrangements for Jess's bachelorette party.

Maybe after that she could persuade Jack back into bed...

Jess! Jess and Luke! Oh, *man*! She'd forgotten that she was having lunch with them. She picked up her watch from the dresser and cursed again. She had barely ten minutes before they were due to pick her up. This was Jack's fault and his ability to make her forget everything when his clever hands were anywhere near her body.

Ellie stomped over to the bathroom and looked into the steam to the stunning body beyond. Tight buns, broad chest, a nice package.... A very nice package that knew exactly what it was doing.... *Concentrate, Ellie!*

'Jack?'

Jack, his head full of shampoo, turned around and lifted one eyebrow. 'Changed your mind? C'mon in. I'll wash your back.'

Ellie gestured to her clothes and tipped her head.

'No—no time. Listen, I just suddenly remembered that I made plans for today.'

She saw the disappointment on Jack's face before he rearranged his features into a blank mask. 'Okay. Have fun.'

Ellie tried not to roll her eyes and failed. 'I'm having lunch with Luke and Jess—I forgot. Want to join us?'

Pleasure, hot and quick, flashed in his eyes. 'Sure.'

Ellie thought she'd push her luck and try to satisfy her curiosity. 'So why won't you tell me about your scar?'

Jack tipped his head back under the stream of water. 'Because it's not important.'

'If it wasn't important then you'd talk about it,' Ellie told him, and sighed when she saw the shutters come down in his eyes. She was beginning to recognise that look. It meant that the subject was no longer up for discussion. Ellie blew out her breath. She'd made sweet love to him all night but that didn't mean she could go crawling around in his head. 'Okay, then, be all mysterious. But hurry up, because they'll be here any moment.'

Jack rinsed out the last of the shampoo, switched off the water and grabbed a towel that hung on the railing. He wrapped the towel around his waist and shoved his hair back from his face. Catching Ellie watching him, he placed his hand on her shoulder and leaned forward to drop a kiss on the corner of her mouth.

'You okay?'

'Fine.'

'Not too sore?' Jack placed his forehead against hers and his hands on her waist.

She was a little *burny* in places that shouldn't burn. 'A little.'

'Sorry.' Jack kissed her forehead and stepped back. 'I'm going to find something to wear. Jeans and open-collar shirt?'

'No, shorts and a T-shirt,' Ellie said, following him out of the bathroom. 'We'll probably end up on the rickety deck of some about-to-fall-down shack...'

Jack pulled a face. 'And that's where we'll eat?' he said, doubt lacing his voice.

'That's where you'll eat the most amazing seafood in the world. Luke knows all the best places to eat up and down the coast,' Ellie replied, and sighed when she heard the insistent pealing of her gate bell. 'That's them—early as usual. I'll see you downstairs.'

'Ellie?'

Ellie turned at Jack's serious voice. Oh, God, what was he going to say?

Jack's smile was slow and powerful. 'Thank you for an amazing night.'

Ellie floated down the steps. Ellie Evans, she mused, sex goddess. Yeah, she could get behind that title.

In the late afternoon Jess and Luke, seeing the old lighthouse a kilometre down the beach, decided that they should take a closer look at the old iron structure. Ellie and Jack, who were operating on a lot less sleep, shook their heads at their departing backs, took a bottle of wine and glasses to the beach, found an old log for a backrest and sat in the sand.

'How are you doing?' Jack asked, pouring wine into a glass and then handing it to her.

Ellie squinted at him. 'I'm utterly exhausted. I think we got about two hours' sleep.'

Jack covered his mouth as he yawned. 'I'm tired too. So, did you have fun?'

Ellie blushed. 'Yes, thanks. You?'

Jack laughed. 'I think the fact that I couldn't get enough of you answers that question better than I could with words.' He watched her face flush again and internally shook his head. Her confidence had really taken a battering at some point and never quite recovered.

'Tell me about your ex.'

Ellie looked as if he'd asked her to swallow a spider. 'Good grief—why?'

'Because I think that he messed up your head—badly. Dented your confidence.' Jack dug his toes into the sand as he looked at her. 'Did he?'

Ellie picked up a handful of sand and let it drift through her fingers. 'S'pose so. Not that I had much to start with.'

'And why would that be?'

Ellie tipped her head at him. 'Jack, you saw me. I was plump and very shy, and standing firmly in the shadow of my famous father—who was everything I wasn't. Good-looking, charming, erudite, confident. Then I went to art school.'

He loved that secret smile—the one that lit her up from the inside out. 'And...?'

'And I flourished. I found something I loved and excelled in. I was happy and the weight fell off me. Boys were asking me out on dates, and although I never went I *was* being asked.'

'Why didn't you go?'

'As I said, I was shy. They asked and I said no and I got the reputation of being hard to get. And, boys being boys, they thought that was cool, so I became more popular, which made me more confident and I finally started dating.'

'Where does the grim gallery owner fit in?' Jack asked, draping a possessive leg over hers.

'He was a friend of one of our final-year lecturers and he came to give a talk to the graduating class. On a whim he said that he'd look at our work in progress. He asked to see my portfolio, said that I had talent and told me look him up if I ever got to London, saying that he might offer me an exhibition.' Ellie watched a crab crawl out of a hole and scuttle towards the waves. 'A couple of months later I did meet up with him in London. We started a relationship and he slowly eroded every bit of confidence I'd worked so hard to acquire.'

'How?'

'My art wasn't up to standard.' Ellie shrugged as thunderclouds built in her eyes.

'Why did you stay with him?'

Ellie bit her bottom lip. 'Because he told me he loved me and said that he'd never leave. The two sentences I'd waited to hear all my life.'

Jack rubbed his eyes. 'Oh, sweetheart.'

'Then, during the little time he spent with me, he started on everything else. Clothes and hair. Weight. My cooking, my friends, my skill in the bedroom.'

Jack felt his mouth drop open with surprise, which was closely followed by the burn of fury. 'He said you were a bad lover?'

'No, he said that I was a damned awful lover and a blow-up doll would be more fun.'

If that...Jack swallowed the names he wanted to call Ellie's waste-of-skin ex. No wonder she'd frozen the other night. No wonder she seemed constantly to second-guess herself.

Ellie dug her bare feet into the sand. 'Merri thinks that he and my father scarred me emotionally.'

Well, yeah. 'What do you think?'

Ellie sipped her wine and dropped back so that her elbows were in the sand. 'Of course they did. I'm scared to get close to people because I don't want to run the risk of getting hurt and I know that they'll leave me. I tend to keep myself emotionally isolated. It's safer that way.'

'Safer isn't necessarily better,' Jack pointed out.

Ellie slanted him a look. 'You do the same thing, Jack Chapman, and don't think you don't.'

'What do you mean?' Jack asked, bewildered by her suddenly turning the tables on him.

'You observe, watch, report and walk away. You don't get involved, so you're as much as an emotional coward as me.'

Jack sighed as her well-made point hit him dead centre. He took a minute to allow his surprise to settle before placing his hand on her knee. 'Maybe I am, El.'

Jeez, he wished he could get the words out. It was a perfect time to tell her that they had no future, that she shouldn't expect anything from him, that he couldn't consider settling down with her—with anyone. That he couldn't afford to take this any deeper, to allow her to creep behind the doors and walls of his self-sufficiency.

Ellie's teasing voice snapped him out of his reverie. 'You awake behind those shades, Chapman?'

'Yep.' Jack hooked his arm around her neck, pulled her to him and dropped a hard kiss on her mouth. 'Just thinking.'

'Careful, you might hurt yourself,' Ellie teased, and yelped when his fingers connected with her ribcage. Her wine glass wobbled in her hand and she dropped it when his other hand tickled her under her arms.

'Jack! You wretch! Stop...please, Jack!' Ellie whimpered, and then her breath hitched.

He realised he was lying on her, her mouth just below his. Tickling turned to passion and laughter turned to need as he plundered her mouth.

Jack felt his heart sink into his stomach as he placed his head in the crook of her neck.

Dammit, Ellie, how am I ever going to find the strength to walk away from you?

'I hate hangovers,' Jack thought he heard Ellie mutter.

She was showered, teeth brushed and dressed, but she still looked headachey and miserable, huddled into the corner of the couch, tousle-haired and exceptionally grumpy. But, amazingly, still so sexy.

'Why did I drink so much last night?' she wailed.

Jack crouched down in front of her and smiled as he handed her a couple of aspirin and some water. 'Hey, in reply to every drunken text you sent at various times throughout the evening I suggested that you stop. You told me that you could handle it.'

'Well, I can't,' Ellie sulked.

'Tough it out, sunshine.'

It had been Jess's hen's party last night and Ellie had hosted the pre-clubbing ritual of cupcakes and champagne. When he'd run down the stairs at eight Ellie had been sitting on the edge of the couch and his eyes had rolled back in his head when he'd seen what she was—almost—wearing: a piece of sparkly scrap material covering her breasts, held in place by strings criss-crossing her back, tight jeans and screw-me heels. She'd pulled back her hair into a severe tail, and with dramatic make-up she'd looked dangerous and sexy.

She'd had 'trouble' written all over her face. He'd decided to leave the house before he carried her upstairs, made her change and lectured her on exactly what the men in the club would think, seeing her in that outfit.

When he'd heard her stumble in—with Jess, Clem Copeland and Maddie—it had been after two. The dogs had wandered upstairs at three, and at three-thirty he'd heard the shouted suggestion of skinny-dipping in the pool. He really deserved credit for not looking.

He'd known he must be getting old when he'd chosen to roll over and go back to sleep rather than spy on hot naked women cavorting in the moonlight.

He grinned as he placed his cup on the coffee table in front of them. Oh, he was enjoying this, he thought as he took the opposite corner of the couch and settled in, his laptop between his crossed knees.

Ellie held her head. 'What's with the computer?' she demanded. 'Oooh, I think there are a hundred ADD gnomes tap-dancing in my head.'

'You and I are going to talk about Mitchell,' Jack said pleasantly.

Ellie groaned. 'No, we're not.'

'Mmm, yes, we are.' Jack looked from his screen to her.

His eyes were alert with intelligence, his fingers steady on the keyboard. He was after a story and she was part of it. 'Jack, please...'

'It's just a couple of questions about your father.'

'Questions I don't want to answer,' Ellie said stubbornly.

'Why not?'

'Because it doesn't change anything!' Ellie shouted, and watched as her head fell off her shoulders and rolled across the room. 'He wasn't there for me, *ever*! He was a drop-in dad, and I loved him far more than he loved me.'

Jack shook his head. 'How old were you when your parents got divorced?'

'Fifteen,' Ellie snapped.

'And how did your mother take it?'

'How do you think? She was devastated.' Ellie leaned forward to make her point, groaned and sank back. 'Do you know she never fell in love again after him? He was her one love. And he brushed us both off like we were nothing...'

Ellie felt a sob rise and ruthlessly forced it down. She'd shed enough tears over her father, her ex, men in general. Hangover or no, she wasn't going to shed any more. But she wanted to. She wanted to tell Jack how much it hurt, how much she wanted to be loved, cherished, protected. She didn't *need* to be—not as she had when she was a little girl—but she still had a faint wish to be able to step into a strong pair of arms and rest awhile.

Like now, when her head felt separated from her body and her stomach was staging its own hostile rebellion.

'So you ran from an emotionally and physically absent father to an emotionally and physically absent fiancé. Why?'

'That's not a question about Mitchell,' Ellie retorted.

'Why, El?'

'Because it's what I deserved! Because my love was never enough to keep someone with me! Because I choose badly!'

Jack sighed. 'Oh, El, that is off-the-charts crap. You had a father who was useless and you had a bad relationship. It doesn't mean that *you* are useless!'

'Feels like it,' Ellie muttered. 'And might I point out that you dig around in my head, throwing questions at me, but you won't answer any of mine?' It wasn't fair that he wanted to delve into her life and emotions and he wouldn't allow her into his.

Jack's hands stilled on the keyboard and he sent her a shuttered look. His sigh covered his obvious irritation. 'What do you want to know?'

'You *know* what,' Ellie muttered. She gestured to his chest. 'Tell me about that scar. How did you get it?'

'Heart transplant,' Jack said, his voice devoid of inflection.

'Excuse me?'

'You heard what I said.'

Ellie sat up, her headache all but forgotten under this enormous news. 'But you look fine.'

'That's because I *am* fine! I've been fine for seventeen years!'

Ooooh, touchy subject. Even more touchy than her father issues. 'Hey, I'm still processing this—just give me a second, okay? How would you like me to react?'

'Well, for starters, I'd like you to take that look of pity off your face!' Jack picked his computer up and banged it down onto the coffee table. 'That's why I don't tell people—because they instantly go all sympathetic and gooey!'

Oh, wait... His sharp, snappy voice was pulling her headache right back.

'Stop putting words into my mouth! I never said that.' Ellie pulled her legs up and rested her chin on her knees, her eyes on his suddenly miserable face. His expression practically begged her to leave the subject alone, but he'd opened the door and she was going to walk on in. 'Why did you need a heart transplant?'

'I caught viral pneumonia when I was thirteen. It damaged my heart.'

'And how old were you when you had the transplant?'

'Seventeen.'

'Geez, Jack.' Ellie wanted to crawl into his lap to comfort him, but knew that any affection right now would be misconstrued, deeply unwelcome.

'Nobody outside of my family knows,' Jack warned her. 'It's not something that I want to become public knowledge.'

'Why not?'

'Because it doesn't define me!' Jack's eyes flashed with irritation.

'If it didn't define you to a certain point then you wouldn't keep it so secret,' Ellie pointed out. 'What's the big deal? So you were sick when you were a kid, and you got a new heart—?' Ellie sat up, curiosity on her face. 'Do you know whose heart you got?'

'Yes. It was another teenager. Killed in a car crash,' Jack said curtly. He nodded to his computer and glared at Ellie. 'Can we get back to the subject on hand?'

'No.' Ellie shook her head. 'I'm still trying to wrap my head around this. So you got viral pneumonia, which damaged your heart, and you were sick for a long time. Then you got a new heart and now you're fine?'

'I take anti-rejection pills every day and make a point of keeping myself healthy. Apart from that, and the scar, I'm as normal as anyone else.'

Physically, maybe, but Ellie suspected that there was a whole bunch of psychological stuff still whirling around in his head. She needed to understand how it had moulded the man in front of her. Because she had no doubt that it had. How could it not have? It was too big, too life-changing—in every sense of the word. 'Tell me about those years between falling sick and having the operation.'

'You're not going to let this go, are you?'

Jack rested his forearms on his knees in a pose she was coming to realise was characteristic of him and linked his hands.

'I became housebound, lacking energy, lacking breath. I got sick frequently. Sport, school, partying, girls were all out of the question…it was an effort just to stay alive. At the end stages just before the op, my heart was so damaged that I could hardly walk. I…*existed*.'

She could hardly imagine it—this vibrant, energetic, amazing man, who should have been an active, lively teen, restricted by his failing heart and deteriorating health. 'Frustration' and 'resentment' were words far too weak to describe some of the emotions he must have experienced at the time.

'And that time defined the rest of your life?'

'Yes.'

'How?'

'I hate being told what I can or can't do, that I have to stay in one place, that I can't pick up and leave. I lived a life of very few choices. I vowed to never limit myself again. For the best part of my teenage life I was so…*confined* that I promised myself I would never be again. And I promised Brent—'

'Who?'

'My donor. I promised him, and myself, that I would *live* life, not exist. Not try to protect myself. That I'd do everything he never had the chance to.'

Phew. Well, she'd asked.

Jack stood up abruptly. 'I need more coffee. Do you want another cup?'

The door slammed shut. Ellie shook her head and wished she hadn't. *Ow, my head!* How was she supposed to take in and think about Jack's monumental disclosure when her head was splitting apart?

No fair.

NINE

____

JACK LEFT THE room and Ellie stared at the spot he'd vacated and forced herself to concentrate. A heart transplant? Was he being serious? Of course he was, she'd seen his scar, but...*holy mackerel*. She'd expected to hear about a big operation, but a heart transplant was a very big deal. How could it not be?

Ellie heard Jack's footsteps behind her and sent him a wary look as he sat down beside her, another cup of coffee in his hand.

'You still want to talk about it, don't you?' Jack asked, his expression stating that he'd rather have his legs waxed.

Ellie leaned back and put her feet up on the coffee table. 'It's just another part of your history—like stitches or breaking a leg...though on a much mightier scale.'

'You laughed when you heard about those incidents. I can handle humour. I can't stand pity.' Jack glared at her.

'Sorry, I'm a bit short on heart transplant jokes,' Ellie shot back. 'And stop glaring at me! I didn't torture you to tell me.'

'You'd be surprised,' Jack retorted, looking miserable. 'I look into your eyes and I want to tell you...*stuff*.'

Ellie batted her lashes and Jack laughed. Reluctantly, but he laughed. 'You appear to be sweet but you are actually a brat, do you know that?'

'Sweet? *Ugh*.' Ellie wrinkled her nose. 'What a description. I prefer "amazing sex goddess".'

Jack's laugh was a lot easier this time. 'You are that too. But you'll have to keep proving it to retain the title.'

Ellie slapped his groping hands away and captured the hand closest to hers. 'I will, but I need to say something to you first.' His expression became guarded at her serious tone, but she decided to carry on anyway. She took a deep breath and spoke. 'I'm sorry for what you lived through but, although you probably won't believe me, I don't feel pity. If anything I'm in awe of what you've achieved, how you've refused to allow your past to limit you.'

Jack shoved a hand into his hair, squirmed, but Ellie ploughed on.

'You could've chosen to protect yourself, to hide out, to nurture yourself, and everyone would've understood. But because you're you you probably said to your heart, *Right, dude, we've both got a second chance. Hang on—we're going for a ride.* Am I right?'

'Yeah...I suppose.'

'I respect the hell out of you. You're also...well...not ugly...which doesn't hurt.'

Jack's laugh whizzed over her head as he reached for her and pulled her across his lap. Ellie looked up at him and swallowed. When she teamed her respect for him with his sharp intellect, his dry sense of humour and the fact that he was a very decent guy, her heart started doing somersaults in her ribcage.

Add their physical chemistry to the mix and she had a soupy mess that could blow up in her face.

Since they'd started sleeping together she'd refused to think of him as anything other than a brief affair. Whenever she found herself thinking about him in terms of more, she reminded herself that she only had tomorrow or the next day or the next and closed the door on those fantasies. She wouldn't think of him in any other context other than that of a short-term, big-fun, no-strings affair, because it would be so easy to allow him to slip inside her heart and her head and that way madness lay. He would leave—he'd told her he would—and she would be left holding her bruised and battered heart.

Jack's thumb brushed over her lips and he just looked down at her with a soft, vulnerable expression on his face that she'd never seen before. It was encounters like this that dragged her deeper into an emotional quagmire. He was so enticing, on both an emotional and physical level, that it was difficult to not slip over the edge into deeper involvement. She was teetering on the edge. But she had to step back...because thinking of anything else was, frankly, stupid.

There were a couple of things she was sure of: she could love him, really love him, but he didn't want or need her love. And he'd never need her, love her, as she needed him to.

Life was tough enough without having to compete with his job for his attention and his time. History had taught her that she'd end up either disappointing him or being disappointed. Both sucked equally, so why risk either? No, falling all the way in love with him was *not* an option, she thought as his mouth drifted across hers.

But it might be easier said than done.

It was the start of a new week and Jack, after spending hours at his computer, chipping away at Mitch's story, felt as if he needed a break. It was the middle of the afternoon so he walked down to the bakery and ducked behind the counter. Sliding behind Samantha, he shoved a mug under the spout and shot a double espresso into a cup. Yanking a twenty out of his pocket, he dropped it in the pocket of her apron and snagged a chocolate muffin before walking through the stable door into the bakery.

As was his habit, he spent a moment admiring Ellie's legs beneath the scarlet chef's jacket before walking over to her table and pulling at the ponytail that fell out of her baseball cap.

Ellie lifted her fondant-full hands, smiled at him and eyed his muffin. 'I'm starving—can I have some?'

Jack held the muffin to her mouth and sighed when Ellie took an enormous bite. 'Piglet.'

'I didn't have lunch,' Ellie explained. 'I got involved in this cake.'

Jack ran his hand down Ellie's back and popped the rest of the muffin into his mouth.

'You have people who slap together sandwiches for your customers not twelve feet from you—order something,' Jack suggested.

'Crazy day,' Ellie told him, and resumed working on a delicate cream rosebud that looked almost real.

He peered over her shoulder at the sugar-rose-scattered wedding cake. 'That's really pretty.'

'Thanks,' Ellie responded, her brow furrowed in concentration as she resumed work rolling a tiny petal.

Jack sat on a stool next to her table and watched her work. Her laptop stood open on the table in front of her and he gestured to it with his coffee cup. 'What's with the laptop?'

Ellie spared it a brief glance. 'I've been trying to talk to my mother about the having-to-move-the-bakery situation and she promised to find a place she could Skype from. I'm waiting for her call.'

Progress of a type, Jack thought, but he doubted that Ellie would share the full responsibility of Pari's with her mother. He could see the tension in the cords of her neck, in her raised shoulders. She didn't want to burden her mum and would find any excuse not to. And if he knew her—and he thought he did—she would downplay the situation she was in.

Sometimes Jack wanted to shake her. She had about five months to purchase the property, do the renovations and move the bakery if she didn't want to lose any trade. She was wasting daylight in so many ways...trying to charm the owner of the building into selling when she should be threatening to walk away...chatting to her mum via Skype when she should have demanded that she return home weeks ago... Jack sighed. He tried to negotiate, rather than confront people, but he could kick ass when he needed to. Ellie's confrontation style was that she didn't essentially *have* one.

Although she *did* have a way of making him emotionally vomit all over his shoes, Jack thought, thinking about their discussion yesterday. He couldn't believe that he'd told her about his operation, his life before he'd started living again. He'd never told anybody—never discussed his past. God, if it wasn't for his mother nagging him about his check-ups he wouldn't discuss it at all.

That would be the perfect scenario. How he wished he could erase the scar, the memories, the feeling that someone had him by the throat every time he thought about it. Ellie didn't understand how difficult talking about it had been for him. He'd felt as if he'd been giving birth while he was sitting on that couch, forcing the words through his constricted throat. He'd been catapulted back seventeen years to a place he'd never wanted to revisit. He'd always been reticent, self-contained, and being so sick had isolated him from his peers and made him more so. He didn't allow people into his mind or his heart easily.

Yet Ellie kept creeping in. Did that mean that they'd moved from being a casual relationship to something that mattered? If so, he sure hadn't planned on that happening...how had that happened? And when?

A day ago...a week ago...the first time he saw her in the bakery?

He'd thought that he'd be able to live with Ellie, sleep with Ellie and remain unaffected...*hah!* And some said he was a smart guy! He shoved his hands into his hair and tugged. Being in Cape Town was becoming a bit too complicated. He felt far too at home here in Ellie's house, among her things. He'd never meant it to be a place where he could see himself living...

Yet a part of him could. Maybe it was Ellie...okay, most

of it *was* Ellie, but it didn't help that she lived in possibly one of the most beautiful places he'd ever seen. Mountains and sea, sunny days, aqua and cobalt water, a pretty town. She had nice friends, people he could see himself spending time with, an interesting job, a relaxed, comfortable house.

It was miles—geographically and mentally—away from his soulless, stuffy flat in London, with its beige walls and furniture...although he *did* miss his kick-ass plasma TV. If he ever moved here that would be the only household appliance he'd pay to ship out here...

Jack gripped the edge of the stool. He was allowing the romance of the setting, his sexual attraction to Ellie and the prettiness of this area cloud his practicality. He was going soft—and possibly crazy.

He needed to go back to work. Needed a distraction from his increasingly sentimental and syrupy thoughts. There was nothing quite like a conflict, a war or a disaster, to slap your feet back to the ground.

Jack's reflections were interrupted by a Skype call coming in on Ellie's computer. At her request, Jack hit the 'answer' button with his non-sticky finger and Ellie's brown-eyed mother appeared on screen. They could be sisters, Jack thought. A couple less laughter lines, long hair instead of short, blue eyes, not deep brown.

'*Namaste*, angel face,' said Ashnee, blowing her a kiss before wrapping her bare arms around her knees and grinning into the camera.

Ellie leaned on her elbows and stared at the screen. 'Mum, I miss you so much. You look fabulous!'

Ashnee fluffed her short hair. 'I feel fabulous. I see that I'm in the bakery. Busy?'

'Hugely,' Ellie said. 'And that's what I need to talk to you about.'

Jack listened as Ellie explained the situation to her mum, and from beside the computer watched the emotions cross Ashnee's face. There was sadness, regret and then resignation.

'And we definitely can't afford the new rent?'

Ellie shook her head. 'Nope.'

Ashnee looked down at her hands, beautifully decorated with henna designs. 'So we have to move? To the old Hutchinson place?'

'Mmm, if only I can get Mrs H to sell.'

Ellie looked up as the stable door opened and lifted her hand to greet Merri who, as per usual, had Molly Blue on her slim hip. She indicated that she was on a call and Merri nodded and wandered over to the table where she usually worked, where two less experienced bakers were making macaroons.

Ellie listened with half an ear as her mum repeated her words back to her. She knew it was Ashnee's way of thinking the problem through, so she half listened and watched the conversation between Merri and the other bakers. Merri looked cross and the bakers frustrated, and when Merri picked up a batch of baked macaroons and tossed them into the dustbin behind them Ellie felt her temper heat.

Merri had no right to do quality control when she wasn't even working on the premises. Right—she needed to sort this out before she ended up with no macaroons and no bakers.

'Mum...' Ellie reached out her hand, grabbed Jack's hard arm and pulled him into the camera's view '...meet Jack. Jack—Ashnee. Jack and I are kind of seeing each other...have a chat while I sort something out.'

'Uh...'

Jack looked from her to the screen but Ellie ignored his panicked face. Good grief, anyone would think she'd asked him to meet the Queen! Ellie rolled her eyes and walked across the bakery. One pair of annoyed and two pairs of mutinous eyes looked back at her.

'What are you doing, Merri?' she asked, keeping her voice low and even.

'The macaroons were lumpy,' Merri stated, allowing Mama Thandi to take Molly from her. Merri placed her hands on her hips. 'That means the mixture was under-mixed.'

Ellie walked over to the dustbin, opened it and grabbed one of the discarded macaroons. It wasn't Merri-perfect but they could have sold the product. And, dammit, Merri had wasted time and energy, electricity and ingredients, when she wasn't even supposed to be at work.

Ellie dropped the pastry back into the bin, closed her eyes and hauled in a deep breath. She felt like an old dishrag, with every bit of energy and enthusiasm wrung out of her. And the two people who'd always been her backstop, her support structure—the other two pillars of the bakery—were wafting in and out or, in her mum's case, wafting around the Indian sub-continent, while she buckled under the responsibility of keeping the bakery afloat.

It was her fault. She'd allowed them their freedom. But enough was enough. She was done, and if they didn't step up she'd collapse under the weight and Pari's would come crashing down.

She would *not* let that happen.

Ellie opened her eyes and as she did so took a step towards Merri, grabbed her wrist and pulled her across the bakery to her table.

'What is *wrong* with you?' Merri demanded when they reached Jack, rubbing at her wrist in irritation.

'You! *You* are what is wrong with me!' Ellie snapped back, and then she pointed her finger to her mum, on the other side of the world. 'And you! Both of you are going to listen to me!'

Jack cocked his head and stepped back. *Clever man*, Ellie thought. Get out of the area about to be firebombed.

'You first.' Ellie looked at Merri. 'You either work here or you don't. You aren't allowed to walk into my bakery if you don't and do quality control.'

'I was just…' Merri's words trailed off.

Huh…Ellie thought. *My scary face is actually scary!* She steeled herself to say what she needed to. 'I love you, Merri, and I desperately want you to come back to work. Next week is the beginning of a new month. Either get your ass back to work on that day or get fired. Have I made myself clear?'

'Ellie, let's talk about this,' Merri replied, in her most persuasive voice.

'We're not talking about anything! That's the way it is. Be here or don't bother coming back.' Ellie held her stare until Merri turned away and flounced off.

Round Two, Ellie thought, and looked down at her mum. This next conversation would be just as hard, if not harder. She bit her lip and looked for the words. 'Mum, I know that I told you to take this time to travel, to live your dream, but I'm yanking you back. I need you here. I cannot do this alone.'

Ashnee looked at her for a long time and Ellie held her breath. What if she said no? Refused to give up her travelling? What would she do then? Ellie felt panic rise up in her throat at her mum's long silence. Just when she didn't think she could stand it any more Ashnee's huge smile filled the screen.

'Oh, thank God!'

Ellie blinked once, shook her head and blinked again. What was she so excited about?

'I didn't think I could stand another minute!' Ashnee cried. 'I've been desperate to come home! I'm sick of the heat and the crowds.'

'But... But...' Ellie looked at Jack, who was quietly laughing, obviously enjoying every minute of this drama. 'I don't understand.'

'Me neither!' Ashnee said cheerfully, dropping her bare feet to the floor. 'All I know is that I'm catching the first plane I can. Which might take a couple of days, since I'm somewhere near nowhere.'

Ellie sat down on her chair and looked bemused. 'Okay. Good. This is a bit overwhelming.'

'Love you, baby girl!' Ashnee blew her a kiss. 'I'll e-mail you as soon as I have some flight deets.'

And with a wink and a grin her mum was gone.

Ellie stared at the screen for a moment longer before

looking up and around. Her mum was gone and Merri was nowhere to be seen. She rubbed her hands over her face, feeling slightly sick at her actions and her words. The impulse to go after Merri was overwhelming...what if she didn't come back? Ellie half stood and felt Jack's strong hand pushing her back into the chair.

'Don't you *dare* go running after her.'

Ellie looked up into Jack's laughing eyes and hauled in a deep breath. 'What have I done?' she whispered.

'Something you should've done ages ago,' Jack replied. He hooked a friendly arm around her neck and chuckled. 'And I have to say...when you finally decide to kick ass you don't take any prisoners.'

A few evenings later Jack wandered into the kitchen as Ellie took a plastic container from the fridge and placed it on the counter. After kissing her hello and getting a lukewarm response he sent her a keen look, trying to work out what was wrong—or more wrong than usual. He knew that she was super-stressed at work, and he suspected that their undefined relationship added another layer of tension to her.

They were reaching a tipping point, he realised. Soon one of them would have to fish or cut bait.

Leaning his forearms on the counter, he peered through the clear lid at tuna steaks covered in a sticky-looking marinade. In the past couple of weeks he'd had more home-cooked meals than he'd eaten since he left home, and fresh fish, properly done, was a treat he never tired of.

Ellie rolled her head and he knew that the knots in her neck were super-tight. 'Spit it out, El. What's wrong?'

'Apart from the normal?' Ellie tipped her head back and looked at the ceiling. 'Horrible day.'

'What happened?'

Ellie placed a strange vegetable on the wooden board and removed a sharp knife from the block of knives close by. He didn't recognise the vegetable and wrinkled his nose.

'Bok choy cabbage. It's good for you,' Ellie stated.

'If you say so. Your day?'

Ellie tossed the cabbage into a frying pan. 'Psycho bride, late deliveries, flood in the upstairs toilet. Samantha wrenched her ankle. Elias is sick.' Ellie took a huge sip of the wine he handed her and sighed with pleasure. 'I need this.'

Ellie pushed a tendril of hair back from her face as she heated another pan for the tuna. Working quickly and competently, she took the tuna steaks to the stove and tossed them into the hot pan. 'Will you get some spring onions out of the fridge, please?'

The steaks sizzled and the room was filled with the fragrant aromas of soy sauce, ginger and garlic. Grabbing his own knife, Jack sliced up the spring onions and asked her where she wanted them.

'In the pan with the bok choy,' Ellie replied. 'Can you get plates?'

Jack handed her the plates as directed. 'Did you manage to get to chat to your mum about the new premises at all?'

Ellie rubbed her eye with her wrist. 'I took her to see

the place and showed her the plans that James the architect drew up. She likes it—likes the building, the plans. I'm not quite sure if it's the travelling or the jet lag or her spiritual journey, but she shrugged off the issue of me not having enough money in my trust fund to buy the building at Mrs H's price and do the renovations, insisting that it'll all work out.'

Ashnee had smiled, hugged her and told her that she just had to have faith—a commodity Ellie had run out of a long time ago.

She was also on the brink of losing her mind, and her life was a pie chart of confusion. The segment labelled 'Jack' was particularly large. Ellie looked at him, sitting at the kitchen table, savouring his wine, his long legs stretched out and his bare foot tickling a dog's neck. She knew that she had only days, maybe hours left with him, and every time she tried to envisage life without Jack in it, her breath hitched in her throat.

She'd never felt fear like this before... What she felt for him terrified her... This was true fear, being confronted with a life without Jack in it. He was only ever supposed to be a fling...when had he turned into someone so damn important? Someone she thought she was in love with?

Thought? Bah! Someone she was horribly, unconditionally, categorically in love with. Dammit...he had her heart in his hands and she knew that when he left he'd drop-kick it over a cliff. It was going to hurt like hell.

Ellie shoved her fist into her sternum and hoped like hell that she was confusing what she was feeling with indigestion. Well, she could always hope...

Ellie quickly plated the tuna steaks and sprinkled sesame seeds over the bok choy before putting them onto the plates.

She gestured to his plate. 'Eat. It's getting cold.'

Jack, looking thoroughly healthy and relaxed, eagerly took her advice and concentrated on his supper, which he ploughed through. He caught her look of amazement at his empty plate. She was barely halfway through hers.

'Hungry?'

'For food like that? Always.' Jack stood up and helped himself to the last piece of tuna steak and the other half of the bok choy cabbage.

'By the way, your mum phoned the bakery today, looking for you.'

Jack lifted his head and frowned. 'What? Why?' He picked up his mobile and shook his head. 'My mobile has a signal. What did she want?'

Ellie smiled. 'That's the odd thing...nothing, really. We had a perfectly pleasant chat about the bakery and what I do and...'

'And she was sussing you out. I told her I was staying with you.' Jack leaned back in his chair and sighed, frustrated. 'Sorry—only child, doubly over-protective mother because I was so sick for so long. She nursed me through it all and can't quite cut the apron strings.'

'I enjoyed chatting to her. Luckily I can talk and ice at the same time, because it was a long call. She said to remind you about Brent's memorial service. He's the donor of your heart, isn't he?'

'Mmm. He died when he was seventeen. It's been seventeen years...'

'Your mum said to let his family know if you can go.

She said that they'd understand if you were on assignment.'

'That's code for *we'd rather not have you there*,' Jack sighed. 'It's a gracious invite, but I suspect that seeing me would be incredibly difficult for them. I imagine they'd feel guilty for wishing he was alive and not me. *I* feel guilty for being alive...'

'Oh, Jack.' Ellie rested her chin on her fist. 'Survivor's guilt?'

'Yeah. Are you going to say something pithy about me not needing to feel that?'

'I wouldn't dare. How could I, not having walked in your shoes?' Ellie toyed with her fork. 'So, are you going to go?'

Jack's eyes flickered with pain. 'I really don't know. But I do know that I have to be back at work some time next week.'

'Ah.' Ellie felt a knife-point deep in her heart. So he'd be gone within the week? Her heart stuttered and faltered and felt as if it would crumble. She had only days more with him. Days to make enough memories to last her a lifetime.

'El, don't look at me like that.'

'Like what?'

'Like you wouldn't say no if I took you right now,' Jack replied.

Ellie cocked her head, pretending to think as heat spread into her womb. She had such limited time to make memories that would have to last her a lifetime so she figured she might as well start immediately. 'I wouldn't say no.'

Jack's eyes widened and Ellie laughed at his shocked face.

'You're joking,' he said, his voice laced with disappointment.

Ellie fiddled with the edge of her top and sent him a slow smile. 'What if I'm not?'

Jack's fork clattered to his plate. 'I think my heart just stopped.'

He lifted his hand, leaned across the table and, as per usual, pushed back a strand of hair behind her ear. Ellie shivered as his finger rubbed the sensitive spot there and trailed down her neck.

'No going back, Ellie. Right here, right now,' Jack muttered, his eyes on her mouth.

Ellie leaned back in her chair and grinned at him as she pulled her tank top over her head to reveal a white, semi-transparent lacy bra.

Jack clutched his chest. 'Heart attack imminent.'

She stood up and walked around the table, standing in front of him while she undid the button that held her soft wraparound skirt together.

'Well, I will slap you later for joking about that—right after I've had my way with you.'

Jack's eyes dropped as the skirt fell to a frothy puddle on the floor, showing her amazing long legs and the smallest scrap of white lace. Placing his hands on her hips, he turned her around. His finger traced the line of her underwear.

'Good God, I'm a goner,' he muttered, placing his mouth on the sensitive dip where her spine met her bottom.

'No, but you will be,' Ellie promised as she turned back.

She gave him an impish look. 'Are you game to see how much this table can actually take?'

'Next week' was here. Despite her not wanting it to, it had crept stealthily and inexorably closer and had finally arrived. Despite her every effort Ellie had not been able to hold back time, and Jack was booked on a flight to London later that morning.

It was time to face reality, pay the piper, face the music, bite the bullet...to stop using stupid idioms.

Jack's clothes were on her bed, his toiletries were in a bag and not on her bathroom shelves, and he was preparing to walk out of her life. Ellie sat on the edge of her bed, sipping a cup of coffee she couldn't taste and wondering what to say, how to act.

It was D-day and she knew that she would have to break through the uneasy silence or else choke on the words that she needed to verbalise. Because if she didn't she was certain she'd regret her silence for ever.

He was too important, too crucial to her happiness for her to let him waltz away without discussing what he meant to her, what she thought they had. Courage, she reminded herself, was not an absence of fear but acting despite that fear.

She had to do this—no matter how scary it was, how confrontational it could become, he was worth it. She was worth it. *They* were worth it.

Too bad that her knees were knocking together and her teeth were chattering. She'd practised this, she reminded herself—had spent the past few nights lying awake, holding him, while the words she wanted to say ran through her head.

All she could remember of those carefully practised phrases was: *I'm in love with you* and *Please don't leave me.*

Ellie put her coffee cup down on the floor next to her feet and crossed her legs. She sat on her hands so that he wouldn't see how much she was shaking.

'Jack...'

Jack looked at her and she sighed at his guarded expression. 'Mmm?'

'Where to from here?' Ellie asked. She winced, hearing the way that the words ran into each other as she launched them out of her mouth.

She saw him tense, caught his jaw hardening. He picked up a pile of shirts and shoved them into his rucksack. 'Between you and I? Ellie, I'm coming back. I mean, I'd like to come back between assignments. To you.'

Well, that was better than him saying goodbye for ever, but it wasn't quite enough. Ellie sucked in her bottom lip. 'Why?'

Jack's eyes flashed in irritation. She could see that he'd been hoping to avoid this conversation. *Tough luck, Chapman.*

'What kind of question is that?'

'A very reasonable one,' Ellie replied. 'Why do you want to come back?'

'Because there's something cooking between us!'

Ellie stood up and walked over to the window, staring out at the sunlight-drenched garden. '"Something cooking between us"? Is that *all* you can say?' Ellie demanded.

'I don't know what you want me to say!' Jack was quiet

for a long time before he spoke again. 'Okay...I've never felt as much for anyone as I do for you.'

Ellie shook her head and her ponytail bounced. Seriously? That was all he could come up with? Where had her erudite reporter gone—the one who relied on words for his living? Where had he run away to?

Well, if he wasn't going to open up she would have to. *Courage, Ellie.*

'Jack, this has been one of the best times of my life. I've loved having you here, with me. I don't want it to end but I am also not prepared to put my life on hold, waiting for you to drop back in.' She pulled in a breath and looked for words, hoping to make him understand her point of view. 'I can't spend my life wondering if you're alive or dead, worrying about you constantly. I don't want to deal with crappy signals and brief telephone calls and even briefer visits home. Living a half-life with you, missing birthdays and anniversaries and special days!' Ellie stated. 'I've lived that life. I hated that life.'

'That was your father, not me! Stop judging me by what he did and said. We are nothing alike!' His expression was pure frustration. 'I am not your father and I don't make promises I can't keep! When I say I'll do something, I'll *do* it. And might I point out that technology has made it a lot easier to stay connected.'

Ellie sent him an enquiring look.

'We have mobiles with great coverage, and when I can't get a signal on my mobile I'll have a satellite phone. I could be on Mars and still be able to call you. There is internet access everywhere, and we could talk every day—hell, every hour, if that's what you needed. And I couldn't survive only seeing you every six weeks. A week, two at the most, and I'd be home.'

'But you can't *guarantee* that!' Ellie shouted.

'Nobody can, Ellie! But I'll do my damnedest!'

Ellie swallowed. She wanted to believe him. She really did. And she believed that he believed it—right now. But without a solid commitment, a declaration of love and trust, it couldn't last. Long-distance relationships, especially those tinged with danger, had a finite lifespan. If he couldn't make a commitment then she had to let him go now, while she could. Now—before she completely succumbed to the temptation of heaven and hell that loving him would be.

Heaven when he came back; hell when he was away.

No, that grey space in between the two, purgatory, was the safest place for her to be. It was the only place where she could function as a semi-normal person.

Ellie shook her head. 'I'm sorry, a mostly long-distance relationship is not an option. I...can't.'

Jack threw up his hands. 'I don't understand why not.'

'Because all you've told me so far is that I am somewhat important and that you'll come back when you can. How can you ask me to wait for you when that's all you can give me?'

Jack pushed both his hands into his hair and linked his hands around the back of his head, his eyes devastated.

'Ellie, I'm doing the best I can. There's never been anyone who has come as close to capturing my heart as you. Ever. But I won't tell you something you want to hear just because you want to hear it. I'm giving you as much as I am able to. Can't you understand that?'

Oh, God, how was she supposed to resist such a naked, emotion-saturated statement? But she had to. There was too much at stake.

'It's not enough for me, Jack. It really isn't.'

'Ellie—'

Ellie held up her hand. 'Wait, let me get this out.' When she spoke again her voice was rich with emotion. 'Over the past couple of weeks I've come to realise—*you* taught me!—that I'm worth making sacrifices for. I think *you* are worth making sacrifices for. But the reality is that you're the one who would always be leaving. I can't force you to change that, I can't force you to need me, and I certainly can't force you to love me. All I can be is a person who can be loved, and I am. I know that now. I want it all, Jack. Dammit, I *deserve* it all!'

'You're asking me to give up my career—'

'I've never asked you to do that. I'm asking you to look at your life, to adjust it so that there is space for me in it. I'm asking you to make me a priority. I'm asking for some sort of commitment.'

Jack's voice was low and sad when he spoke again. 'I need to be able to move, Ellie, breathe. I can't live a humdrum life. I can't be confined—even by you.'

'It's not good enough, Jack. Not any more.' Ellie felt her heart rip out of her chest. 'I can't be with someone who thinks life with me would be humdrum, tedious, boring.'

'I didn't mean—'

'Yes, you did!' Ellie shouted, suddenly pushed beyond her limits. 'You want to think that a life with me would be unexciting and dull because anything else would mean that you would have to get emotionally involved, take a stand, make a choice that could lead to pain. Don't you think you're taking this protecting-your-heart thing a bit too far? You've stopped *living*, Jack.'

'Of course I'm living! What the hell do you think I've been doing for the past seventeen years?' Jack roared, his eyes light with fury.

'That's not living—it's reporting! Living is taking emotional chances, laughing, loving.' Ellie shoved her hands into her hair. 'I'm in love with you and I'm pretty sure that you're the man I can see myself living the rest of my life with. Would you consider loving me, living with me, creating a family with me?'

He stared at his feet, his arms tightly crossed. His body language didn't inspire confidence.

'This is emotional blackmail,' Jack muttered eventually, and Ellie closed her eyes as his words kicked her in the heart. And here came the pain, roaring towards her with the force of a Sherman tank.

'I'm sorry that you consider someone telling you that they adore you blackmail. Goodbye, Jack.' Ellie turned away and folded her arms across her torso, gripping hard. 'Lock the front door behind you, will you?'

'Ellie—'

Ellie whirled around, fury, misery and anger emanating from every pore. 'What? What else is there to say, Jack? I love you, but you're so damn scared of feeling anything that you won't step out of that self-protecting cocoon you've wedged yourself into! Of the two of us, *you* are the bigger pansy-assed coward and I am done with this conversation. Just leave, Jack. Please. You've played basketball with my heart for long enough.'

She heard him pick up his pack, jog down the stairs. From behind the curtain of the bay window Ellie watched him storm to his car, his broad shoulders tight and half-way up to his ears, his arms ending in clenched fists.

I love you, she wanted to say. *I love you so much it scares me. I wish you knew how to take a real chance, how to risk your very precious heart.*

But two sentences kept tumbling over and over in her head. *Please don't leave me. Please come back.*

But he didn't stop, didn't turn around. When she saw his car back down her driveway and watched the tail-lights disappear down the road and out of sight, Ellie sank to the floor and buried her face in her hands.

It was over and she was alone. Again.

TEN

FIVE DAYS AFTER he'd left Cape Town Jack and his cameraman were standing next to a pile of rubble that had once been a primary school on the outskirts of Concepción, Chile. What had originally been a black car was buried under a pile of rocks. A massive earthquake had hit the region and Jack had been asked if he'd like to report on it. He hadn't even left transit at Heathrow. He'd just caught the first flight he could to Chile.

Behind them were mounds of bricks and twisted iron and the half-walls of the decimated school. Since the quake had struck early in the morning most of the children hadn't arrived yet for lessons, but Jack knew from talking to the family members who stalked the site that there had been an early-morning staff meeting and there were still a few teachers unaccounted for. Their relatives were still digging through the rubble, slowly moving piles of bricks to find the bodies of their loved ones. Few held out any hope for their survival. The devastation was too widespread, too intense, for hope to survive for long.

Jack rubbed his hands over his face as he prepared to link live to New York. He didn't want to be here, he thought. He wanted to go home to that bright house with its eclectic art and two rambunctious dogs. He wanted to run with the dogs on the beach, stretch out on the leather couch, listen to the sea at night and the wind in the morning.

He wanted Ellie.

But Ellie would mean giving this up, Jack reminded himself. He couldn't...this was what he did, what he was. He needed to work.... Jack blew out his breath. But was that just years of habit talking? He couldn't avoid the truth...he *needed* her. As much as his work. More.

Jack leaned back against a dusty car and lifted his head to the sunlight. He'd been seventy degrees of dim that last night in St James. He'd thought he was so strong, so in control. While she'd launched those emotional arrows at his soul he'd kept telling himself that it wouldn't hurt, that he'd be fine. Now, five days and too much horror later, he felt as if he'd taken a series of punches to his stomach and heart. He was doubled over in pain.

He was generally level-headed and unemotional, and in truth he'd never been a crier. He could count on one hand the amount of times he'd wept since he was a child. Even the bleakest times of his illness, the fear he'd felt when he'd had the transplant and the relief of being normal again had never reduced him to tears, but the fact that he'd lost Ellie had had him choking down grief more than once or twice. The early hours of the morning were the worst; that was when he felt as if his heart was being physically yanked from his chest.

What was he going to do? Sacrifice his job for her? Sacrifice her for the job? Be bored with a normal life with Ellie in it or miserable with an action-packed existence without her?

He didn't know—couldn't make a decision. All he was certain of was that he missed her, that his world had gone from bright colours to monochrome, that he was plodding through each day feeling adrift without his connection to her. He was fine physically. Mentally and emotionally he was a train wreck. He felt as if he'd been stripped of all his internal organs—heart included—that he was just a shell of a man, marking time.

Ted, his cameraman, told him he was about to go live so Jack stood up straight and waited for the signal. He greeted the anchorwoman and launched into his report. Death, destruction, the cost of rebuilding people's lives...

Jack was midway through when a commotion from the decimated building behind him caught his attention. He knew that noise—it was an indication that someone had been found. Still live to New York, he bounded with Ted over the rubble to where a lone man, his face ravaged with grief, was furiously tossing bricks and stones off a pile. Jack recognised his look of terrible excitement, of despair-ravaged hope. He'd found someone he loved...

Jack, forgetting that he was live on international TV, picked up his pace and scuttled across the rubble to where the man was sinking into a hole he'd dug. Jack saw a strand of long black hair flowing around a half-sheared brick and his heart stopped. He swallowed. It was exactly the shade of Ellie's hair...

The young man was sobbing as he yanked debris away

from her. '*Mi esposa, mi esposa,*' he muttered frantically, tears streaming down his face.

His wife. All he could see was his wife's hair...

Jack swallowed and jumped into the small hole with him, started to throw bricks, planks and stones away from where he imagined her head and body was. The problem was that her hair was so long—she could be lying in any direction.

Minutes felt like hours and his back muscles and biceps were screaming in pain. His shirt was soaked onto his body but Jack refused to quit. There was no sound coming from the victim but Jack knew that didn't mean she was dead. He refused to believe she was dead...

What if this was Ellie? How would he be feeling? The thought kept hurtling through his brain. Desperate, out of control, terrified. He wouldn't be able to live without her...

Jack lifted a board up and away and there she lay, her beautiful face unmarked by the falling building. Her eyes were open, glassy, but Jack didn't need to check her pulse to see that she was still alive. The hand lifting up towards the young man was a solid enough hint.

Jack yelled at Ted to call for the medics and was surprised to see that Ted was still filming. Why wasn't he helping them? Surely the woman was more important than the story? He felt sickened by Ted's callousness, the fact that he could just observe and not participate, to report but not become involved.

Then again, he couldn't blame him either. Wasn't that what *he* did, story after story, situation after situation?

Jack caught the bottle of water someone threw down,

cracked the seal and gently poured a tiny bit of water into the woman's mouth. He didn't want to lift her neck, he had no idea what injuries she had, and her legs were still pinned beneath the debris. Her husband had his face buried in his hands, sobbing uncontrollably.

Jack gently dripped water from the bottle into her mouth and they waited. The young man was now talking to his wife, and Jack felt the lump in his throat grow as he watched them interact, listened to their conversation. It was blindingly obvious that they loved each other so much, that they were ecstatic to be given a second chance.

All his life he'd avoided love, thinking that it equalled confinement. That he'd lose his freedom. That a love affair would hamper his individuality and compromise his independence. He now realised that, compared to losing Ellie, none of it meant a damn thing. His feelings for her scared him, but he knew he was a better man for loving her and that she was worth any emotional risk. He'd been so careful to control every aspect of his life and it was a revelation to discover that being out of control was the best feeling in the world. Being in love felt marvellous. He loved the way it made him feel...

With her he'd found the place he most wanted to be—the home he'd thought he didn't need. She was the one person, the one place, where he could be truly intimate and feel safe. Secure. Looked after. Loved. She had given him the gift of balance and stability and his throat swelled with emotion. He needed to get back to her...

Jack wet the corner of his T-shirt and wiped the victim's face. He saw relief and gratitude in her eyes.

'*Muchas gracias,*' she whispered between dry and swollen lips.

Jack swallowed, nodded and ran his hand over his head as he heard the rescue workers and medics approaching. He sent her a quick smile and backed away, lifting himself out of the small area to allow for medical assistance.

It was only as he walked away from them and Ted that he realised that his face and cheeks were wet with tears.

Across the world Ellie worked in her bakery, waiting for her staff to come in to work. Her heart was haemorrhaging, she decided, as a lone tear dripped off her chin and landed on the pale pink wedding cake beneath her. It had been nearly a week since Jack had left and she missed him with an intensity that astonished her. The memory of the night he'd left was on constant replay in her head, and she relived the moment of her heart ripping apart on a daily, hourly basis, causing pain to shoot through her system. There was no relief from the memories. Every room in the house made her think of Jack, and she hadn't been able to eat at her kitchen table since he'd left.

She wasn't eating, wasn't sleeping, wasn't thinking. Her hands shook. She felt constantly cold. Ellie looked at the tiny tearstain on the cake and felt grateful she could cover it with a sugar rose. Idly she wondered if she should be making wedding cakes with a scorched heart. Wedding cakes should be made with love and hope, not with sadness and regret.

Ellie looked up to see Merri in front of her, dressed in a bright pink apron. 'Reporting for duty, ma'am.'

Ellie just managed to smile. She'd totally forgotten her

threat to fire her if she didn't arrive for work, and now a part of her wished Merri *hadn't* come back, so that she would be so busy she'd never have to think, feel, again.

'It's about time,' Ellie muttered, and held out her arms for a hug.

She stepped into her friend's arms and hung on. After a while she stepped back, felt Merri's hand between her shoulderblades and turned her head to look into her deeply concerned face.

'You okay?' Merri asked.

'Jack left.' Ellie shook her head and wiped her eyes with the corner of her apron. 'I can't seem to stop hurting. I think I'm okay, then it sneaks up on me and *wham*! Dammit—I'm dripping again.'

'God, El, how long have you been like this? Why didn't you call me?'

Ellie winced, feeling the headache pounding between her eyes. 'I couldn't—can't—talk about him.' She bit her lip. 'I feel like I've been eviscerated with a butter knife.'

'Oh, sweetie. You're fathoms deep in love with him.'

Ellie nodded.

Merri sat down on the chair next to Ellie's table and sent her a sympathetic look. 'I'm sorry you couldn't make it work, but sometimes love just isn't enough.'

'It's supposed to be,' Ellie whispered.

Merri's voice was laced with regret and loss. 'In books and movies. In real life...? Not so much.'

Ellie stared past Merri's head. 'I'm worried about him. My imagination is in overdrive.'

'Jack knows how to look after himself.' Merri put her arms on the table. Her face was uncharacteristically serious. 'Ellie, I've never seen you so unhinged. I'm worried about *you*.'

'So is my mum.' Ellie stared at her flour-dusted shoes. 'She keeps telling me that I can't live like this, that I have to do something about him...but what can I do? Nothing! He's gone and he isn't coming back.'

'You need to try and relax. Get a decent night's sleep and find a way to work through this.'

'I'm trying—'

'Try harder. If you carry on like this you'll be on antidepressants in a month, in a loony bin in three months.'

'I know that I'm a mess.' Ellie gripped the bridge of her nose with her thumb and forefinger. 'I feel like I am marinating in pain.' She flipped Merri a tiny smile. 'Does that sound desperately melodramatic?'

'Yes, but you're entitled.'

Merri draped an arm across her shoulder and they both looked down at the wedding cake. Merri tipped her head so that it touched Ellie's. 'Sweetie, I'll be here to hold your hand every step of the way, to talk to you and to cry with you. But this cake...?'

'What's wrong with it?'

Merri picked up a swatch of fabric off the table and held it against the cake. 'Wrong shade of pink, honey.'

Jack shoved his hands into his coat pockets as he left the church where Brent's memorial service had just ended. It was over, and yet he didn't feel the relief he'd expected to. He'd delayed his return to Cape Town to be here but he wondered if he'd ever manage not to feel guilty for being alive. He needed to get to Ellie. She'd understand, help him work through this.

Now he needed to avoid the Sandersons if he could. What could he say to them? He was sorry? He was...but it sounded stupid, seeing that he lived because Brent had died. There they all were—Mrs Sanderson hugging his mother by the gate, Mr Sanderson, his eyes pink from cold and tears, talking to his dad.

He should say something. Anything... But he really just wanted to walk away. They couldn't—wouldn't—want to talk to him.

Jack had made it halfway to his car when he heard his name being called.

'Jack!'

He felt the hand on his arm, turned and looked down into Brent's mother's elegant face. He winced internally.

'Where are you rushing off to?' she asked.

Jack, guilt holding his heart in a vice grip, looked around for a means of escape. 'Uh...'

'I'm so glad you came. *We're* so glad you came.'

Oh, Lord, now Mr Sanderson had joined them. Any moment his parents would join the party and he'd be toast. Jack forced himself to put his hand out and shake Mr Sanderson's hand. 'Sir. It was a nice service.'

'We're very happy you made it, Jack. And call me David.'

'I'm June.'

Oh, this was getting to be fun. *Not*. Jack jammed his freezing hands back into his coat pockets and reluctantly nodded when David asked him if he'd take a short walk with them through the cemetery. Jack sent his mother a miserable look over his shoulder and followed Brent's parents to Brent's headstone. June dusted some snow off the face of the stone and rested her gloved hand on top.

'We've wanted to talk to you for a while. We've been following your career,' David said. 'You've made quite a name for yourself.'

'Thank you.'

'You didn't want to come today,' June said. 'You didn't want to see us. Why not?'

Jack looked at a point beyond her face. 'I thought it would hurt you too much.'

'And? Come on—spit it out,' June coaxed.

Her eyes encouraged him to be honest, and for a moment he felt as if he was seventeen again and terrified.

'And it kills me to know that Brent had to lose his life so that I could have mine,' Jack said in a rush, scared that if he didn't get the words out he never would.

June's eyes filled with tears and her face softened. 'Sweetheart, his death had nothing to do with you. It was his time to go...'

'But—'

'But nothing. I'm just grateful that you had a second chance at life. Grateful that you haven't wasted his gift...' June took his hand between hers. 'Yet your mother tells us you have no home, no family, no partner. It worries her. It worries *us*. Why not?'

'Uh—'

'When we gave you our son's heart we expected you not to waste your second chance. We also expected you to make the most of your second chance,' David stated, his voice firm but gentle. 'But we never wanted you to feel guilty—only thankful.'

His mother must have had more than a few discussions with them about him for them to be having this conversation, Jack realised. He wasn't sure whether to be grateful or to wring her neck for interfering. He smiled inside. He'd go for grateful.

'So you think it would be okay if I fell in love? Had a family? Even knowing that Brent never had that chance and I do, with *his* heart?' he asked, holding his breath.

David placed his hand on his shoulder and squeezed. 'Not only do we think it's okay, we think it's important. It's another chance—another opportunity for you to be fulfilled—and that's all we ever wanted. For you to make the most of his gift, to wring out as much happiness as you can from life. Brent had a generous spirit and that would be his wish.'

'And it's ours...' June added.

Jack swallowed the tears he felt at the back of his throat as their words picked up the last of his guilt and flew away with it. He managed what he suspected was a watery grin. 'Well, there is this girl, and she's been giving our heart a run for its money...'

June grinned and put her hand into the crook of his elbow. 'Ooh, a feisty one. I like her already.'

Three days later Ellie sat cross-legged in the middle of the driveway and gazed at what she was privately calling Ellie's Folly. Fascinated, she rested her elbow on her knee and her chin in her hand and just looked. The house preened in the spotty sunlight that appeared now and again from between low black clouds, like an elderly showgirl remembering her former life.

Rolled up and sticking out of the back pocket of her shorts was the agreement of sale that Mrs H had finally signed an hour before.

'*Enough is enough,*' *she'd told Mrs H, after carefully explaining what she intended doing with the property.* '*Either accept my offer or I'm walking away.*'

'*But—*'

'*Permanently. Pari's will close down, jobs will be lost and St James will lose a landmark institution. I'm tired of your vacillations and games. I'm dealing with enough drama as it is and I don't need any more. The ball is in your court.*'

Getting tough had paid dividends and the old lady had signed at a price that allowed her enough cash to do the renovations. She was now the owner of a gorgeous old building that needed lots of love and attention. Thank goodness—because she seriously needed the distraction of hard work.

It had been a good day. If she ignored the fact that she was still miserable and heartbroken and so, so sad.

Ellie felt something cold nudge her shoulder and looked sideways to see a large frappe in one of Pari's takeaway glasses. She'd told her mum that she'd be here and wasn't surprised by her presence.

'Isn't she stunning?' Ellie breathed, unable to take her eyes off the building.

'She is—but you are even more so.'

Ellie scrambled to her feet as that deep voice caressed her. She looked at him, wide-eyed with astonishment.

Jack was back and he was standing in front of her, looking fit and fantastic.

Ellie took a step back, feeling totally disorientated and more than a little scared. Why was he back? Oh, her battered heart had lifted at the sight of his wonderful face, but how it would hurt when he left again. How would she survive this? Would she ever get used to him dropping in and out of her life?

Yet...she didn't care. After the past days of hell on earth it didn't matter. None of it mattered. Because, as sobering and shocking as the concept was, there was nothing she wouldn't do for him. The reality was that she'd never loved anyone or anything as much as she loved Jack...she would give up Pari's for him, move to the ends of the earth for him...she'd even live through having her insides scraped out with a teaspoon every time he went on a dangerous assignment if it meant having him smile at her, laugh with her, hold her after making love to her.

He was back, she loved him and she'd do anything to be with him.

Ellie dropped her iced coffee to the driveway and only just stopped herself from flinging herself against his chest and weeping like a fool. Instead she put the heels of her hands to her temples and shrugged her shoulders. 'Okay, I surrender.'

'You surrender what?' Jack asked conversationally, his finger tapping his still full cup of coffee.

'Do you want me to leave Pari's? I can make cakes in London. I'll take Rescue Remedy and yoga and meditation classes every time you go on assignments to hellholes. I'll get through it.' Ellie stumbled to the low wall that ran parallel to the driveway, sat down and dropped her head into her hands. 'What do you need me to do?'

'Now, *why* would you do all that, El?' Jack asked.

She felt him sit down next to her. 'Because I love you and I can't live without you,' Ellie muttered to the concrete. She felt his big hand on the back of her neck as tears dripped onto the paving below.

Jack pulled her head to his shoulder and held it there as he continued to sip his coffee. 'That's a hell of an offer, El.'

Ellie looped her arms around his waist, still staring at their shoes. She sniffed, the reality of what she'd offered slowly sinking in. She'd miss Merri and her staff, her customers and this new building that she'd never have the chance to turn into something special. And her house—she really loved her house—but she'd take her pets. That wasn't negotiable.

She'd miss the beach and the city but she'd have Jack... Her racing heart settled. She'd have Jack sometimes and it would be all right. Anything was better than nothing.

She felt Jack's kiss in her hair before he let her go. Ellie wiped her eyes with the back of her wrist and sniffed.

'I have a counter-offer,' Jack said, his voice vibrating with emotion.

'You do?'

'As it happens, I love you too.' The corners of his mouth kicked up when her mouth fell open. He put his finger under her chin and pushed it up so that her teeth clicked together. 'I can't—won't—ask you to uproot your wonderful life. But I *can* ask you if I can share it.'

There went her jaw again. 'Sorry?'

Jack pulled his feet up, bent his legs and rested his arms on his knees. His cup was on the wall next to his feet. The late-summer breeze blew his hair off his forehead. 'I want to stay here, live in your house with you. On an on-going and permanent basis.'

'Uh—'

Jack managed to grin. 'Work with me here, darling. I'm trying, very badly, to propose.'

'Propose what?' Ellie said blankly, still stuck three sentences behind, on the 'I love you too' comment.

'I can't imagine my life in any form without you in it so...will you marry me?' Jack asked.

'Uh—what?'

'You? Me? Married?'

'You want to *marry* me?' Ellie squawked.

'That's what I keep saying. But the question is, do you want to marry *me*?'

Jack bit his lip, anxiety written all over his face. Ellie couldn't believe that her tough warrior—a man who'd faced untold danger, who'd lived through and overcome so much in his life—was scared of rejection, scared that her answer might be no.

Gathering her last two wits together, she leaned forward and placed her hands on his knees.

'Yes. Absolutely.'

Jack dropped his forehead to his chest in relief and Ellie rubbed her thumbs over the bare skin on the inside of his knees. He was warm and strong and vital and her world suddenly made sense again.

'I *do* love you, El,' Jack muttered, his voice hoarse as he looked at her with blazing eyes.

Her heart constricted and fluttered and, lifting her hands, she gently held his face. 'I love you too. Welcome home.'

Ellie sat sideways between Jack's legs, his arms loosely around her waist and his chin on her head. They'd been quiet for a while after his proposal, both happy to savour the moment.

She didn't want to break the spell, but Ellie knew that they still had a couple of issues to work through. 'What about kids, Jack? Do you want any?'

He looked down at her and half shrugged. 'Sure. When?'

Ellie blinked. 'Excuse me?'

Jack squeezed her waist. 'I don't think you really heard me before, or took in what I said, but I want it all. But it starts with you. If you want kids now, later, whenever... I just want to make you happy.'

Ellie blinked, swallowing as emotion—love—grabbed her heart. 'Oh, you slay me.' She pushed her hair back. 'I'd like your baby, Jack—hell, I'd *love* your baby. But not right now. I'd like us to take a little time for ourselves. Just to *be*, to get used to our new life together, before we throw another person into the mix.'

'We can do that.' Jack pulled up her T-shirt and put his warm hand on her bare skin.

Ellie shivered at his touch and hoped that she never stopped responding like this.

She tipped her head back and sideways to look up at him. 'You said that you just want me to be happy but

I want *you* to be happy—how are we both going to be happy?'

Jack let out a joyful laugh. 'You really didn't hear me earlier, did you?'

Ellie blushed. 'I kind of tuned out after you told me you loved me. Tuned back in when you proposed. In between it's a bit blurry.'

Jack scooted backwards so that he could look down into her face. He was hers—a warrior soldier with a scarred body, warm smile and vulnerability in his eyes.

'Okay, are you concentrating?'

Ellie laughed. 'Jack!'

'El, I love it here—love your dogs, your city, your friends. I'm happier here than anywhere else.' He ran the edge of his thumb over her trembling bottom lip. 'I've been a fighter all my life but I'll fight hard for you—fight to share your sunshine-filled life.'

'But your career—'

Jack shrugged. 'I still want to do parts of it—with your support. But I can pick and choose my stories a bit better. I don't always need to go into hot areas, chase the conflicts. I can do human drama stories, crime, special reports. I might have to go away now and again, but I meant what I said. There are ways for us to communicate every day and I wouldn't want to be away from you for long.'

Ellie swallowed. How long was long? 'A month? Two?'

Jack laughed. 'Are you mad? I couldn't survive that long without you! A week—maybe ten days at the most. And that would be pushing it.'

Ellie grinned. Jack was not going to be an absent husband, a forgetful lover. He was right. He was nothing like her father.

She tapped his knee in warning. 'Do *not* get hurt again.'

She felt his lips smile against hers. 'Deal.'

Ellie toyed with his fingers. 'But, Jack, if you need to go into a situation that's dangerous, I meant what I said. I'll find a way to deal with it. I don't want you to miss it or feel cheated.' She needed him to understand. 'You were right. You are nothing like my dad or my ex. And I am nothing like that shy, plump insecure little girl. I can cope with you being away for short periods as long as we keep communicating...'

'Don't think this is only from your side. I need to connect with you as well, sweetheart. I missed you so much when I was in Chile. I felt...*bereft*.'

Ellie draped her thighs over his and scooted closer, so that she could link her hands at the back of his neck. 'Was it bad?'

'Yeah. It was.' Jack nodded.

'I saw the footage of you rescuing that woman,' Ellie said quietly. 'Merri caught it on the news and I downloaded the clip from the internet.'

'I guess they aren't calling me unemotional any more, since I was caught crying on camera.' Jack rubbed his forehead with the tips of his fingers. 'She looked like you. Long black hair, creamy skin. Gorgeous. Her husband was a train wreck and I kept thinking: how would I feel if this was you? Gutted, shell-shocked, scared witless.' Jack frowned. 'I've been scared in my life, El, but nothing compares to how terrified I was when I considered what it would feel like to lose you permanently.' Jack shuddered before he spoke again. 'I went to Brent's service—spoke to his parents.'

'That must have been hard. How was it?'

Jack smiled. 'It was...healing. For all of us. Me especially.'

'I'm so glad.' Ellie's breath hitched. 'I know that you're not into these mushy moments, but I just want to keep telling you how much I love you...'

'I don't mind hearing that.' Jack's mouth kicked up as his hand cradled the side of her head. 'And ditto for me. There's so much I still want to say...'

'Like?'

'Like my world has colour again now that you are back in it.' His eyes turned serious. 'El, I love my work, but I love you more. I'll never cheat on you. I promise to be faithful. And I promise, as far as I'm humanly able, to be here when you need me. I promise to be with you on the important dates, and if and when we have kids I'll look at my career and see what I can change to be an active, involved dad.'

Ellie opened her mouth to speak but Jack shook his head.

'You're my life. You're what makes me happy. I want to wake up next to you, wander down to the bakery for breakfast, be with you at night. Unfortunately I have to earn money, and I do enjoy what I do. But if I have to choose between the two I'll choose you.'

'You don't have to choose.' Ellie gulped as Jack lifted his thumbs to wipe away her tears. His mouth lifted at the corners and his eyes darkened with emotion, and

Ellie caught a glimpse of his soul, overflowing with love for her.

He took her hand and placed it on the left side of his chest. 'I've protected my heart in every way I can. Physically, emotionally, spiritually. It's on loan to me and now I'm giving it to you...this heart that saved my life—it's yours.'

Ellie gulped a sob and the stream of tears that she'd been holding back slid down her face. Leaning into him, she placed her cheek against his, and when she thought she could talk sensibly again she took his hand and echoed his action by putting it on her chest. 'Then take mine. Keep it safe.'

'I promise I will.'

And they both knew, in a way only lovers could understand, that their hearts were joined—married—on that low stone wall outside a decrepit house in the late-afternoon summer sun.

EPILOGUE

———

Six months later

ELLIE FELT HER mum's arm around her
waist as she stood at the edge of the crowd, waiting to be
called by the Master of Ceremonies to make her speech.
Merri stood on her other side, with Molly Blue in her
pushchair, sucking a doughnut.

It was the day of Pari's grand re-opening and the new
building was restored to its formal splendour. The gardens might need a year or two to mature, but spring was
almost upon them and she could see tiny shoots of new
growth on the rescued rose bushes, on the trees and
bushes.

The bakery had been operating for a week and there
had been problems—but nothing insurmountable. Business was booming in the bakery, in the new restaurant,
in the tiny art studio/gift shop she'd set up to display her
artwork and some works by other artists from the area.

She only had one little issue... Her fiancé—the man
she was due to marry in a month—was not yet home. He

was nowhere to be seen. She had no idea why he was delayed because every time she called him his mobile went straight to voicemail, and he'd left his satellite phone at home. She could feel her mum and Merri's rising annoyance—this was her big day and he wasn't here. Ellie knew that her mum was trying to keep back all the 'I told you so' and 'war reporters—consistently unreliable' phrases that she desperately wanted to utter.

Ellie resisted looking at her watch. Jack would get here, and if he didn't he would have a damn good excuse for not being able to make it. Over the past six months he'd done everything he'd said he would and he loved her absolutely, intensely, ferociously. He'd never deliberately hurt her and sometimes things happened. *Life* happened.

'Relax, guys,' Ellie told them, sending them both a great big smile. 'I am.'

'Has he forgotten how to use a phone?' Ashnee demanded. 'I'm really quite annoyed with him—'

'You can read me the Riot Act later, Ash,' Jack said from behind them, and Ellie squealed in delight as she whipped around. 'Right now, I'd like to kiss my girl.'

Then his big hands were cradling her face, his lips were on hers and the tectonic plates deep in the earth shifted and settled. When he finally lifted his head he smiled down at her. 'Sorry—battery on my mobile died. And I got a speeding fine on the way here.'

'I *knew* you would get here on time.' Ellie smiled. 'Missed you.'

'Missed you too,' Jack replied.

Ellie pulled her bottom lip between her teeth. 'How did it go with the cardiologist?'

His heart transplant wasn't a secret any more. It wasn't something he discussed, but it was out in the open. 'Fine—situation normal. He says that you're looking after my heart beautifully.'

Her lips twitched. 'Good.'

'I'm sorry that I had to delay my return. I really wanted to be home sooner. But I decided to wait for your present.'

Ellie held his hand between both of hers. 'My present? What is it?'

Jack's eyes flashed with mischief. 'It's a few things, actually. Two of them are my parents, who insisted on being here for Pari's re-opening.'

Ellie and Ashnee, who'd instantly bonded with Jack's mother Rae, danced on the spot. 'That's fabulous news. I'm so happy they're here. Where are they?' Ellie demanded, looking around at the sizeable crowd.

'Over there. With your other present—Mitch. He flew back from New York with me.'

Jack gestured to the crowd to the right of them and Ellie's heart hitched when Mitchell raised his hand and waved it in her direction. Her dad was here...finally... at one of the most important occasions of her life. Ellie felt her heart stumble. This was Jack's doing, she knew. She *so* appreciated the fact that he'd gone to the effort of getting him here, that he thought that Mitch being here would make her happy. And it did—sort of. She'd invited Mitch but never expected him to come. It was such a relief to know that she didn't need her dad's approval any more; she'd finally accepted that her father wasn't father material and his lack in that department had nothing to do with her.

He was—had been—a shocking father, but she could forgive him anything since he'd sent Jack into her life.

'Thank you.' Ellie rose up on her toes to kiss Jack's mouth.

'Pleasure.' Jack ran a hand over her hair as the Master of Ceremonies began his speech. Jack bent his head to whisper in her ear. 'I love you. I'm proud of what you've done, and it's fabulous. But...'

'But?'

'But keep the speeches short, sweetheart, so that I can pull you into a pantry and kiss the hell out of you.'

'That's all you want to do?' Ellie looked at him and shook her head, eyes dancing. 'Damn, I must be getting boring! Got to watch that...'

Ellie grinned as Jack's shout of laughter followed her all the way to the podium.

True happiness, she decided, really was laughing and living and loving well. She tossed Jack a grin as she launched into her very, very, *very* short speech.

After all, she had her man to kiss...

* * * * *

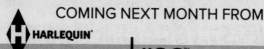
Available September 17, 2013

#33 LAST GROOM STANDING
The Wedding Season • by Kimberly Lang

Having watched her three closest friends all find love, Southern belle Marnie Price feels as if she's the only single girl left. Luckily she's found a solution—one sizzling night with Dylan Brookes. This man wears a wedding tux better than anyone, but all Marnie wants to do is get beneath it!

#34 WHOSE BED IS IT ANYWAY?
The Men of Manhattan • by Natalie Anderson

Returning home after a daring rescue mission, all James Wolfe can think of is sleep. So he's furious to find a beautiful stranger curled up in his king-size bed! Normally no woman ever gets between his sheets without prior invitation—who does she think she is?

#35 BACKSTAGE WITH HER EX
by Louisa George

Hiding out in the gents' toilet backstage is *not* the way Sasha imagined bumping into her significant ex. Especially when that ex is famously wild rock god Nate Munro! She has a massive favor to ask him, but one glimpse of his sinfully dark eyes and all she can think about is that he's seen her naked!

#36 BLAME IT ON THE CHAMPAGNE
Girls Just Want to Have Fun • by Nina Harrington

Saskia Elwood knows agreeing to Rick Burgess's business proposition would be nothing short of madness. But before she can catch her breath she finds herself swept off to Europe for once-in-a-lifetime experiences. Saskia won't be able to blame the sparks flying between them on the champagne for much longer!

YOU CAN FIND MORE INFORMATION ON UPCOMING HARLEQUIN® TITLES, FREE EXCERPTS AND MORE AT WWW.HARLEQUIN.COM.

HKCNM0913

REQUEST YOUR FREE BOOKS!
2 FREE NOVELS PLUS 2 FREE GIFTS!

YES! Please send me 2 FREE Harlequin® Kiss novels and my 2 FREE gifts (gifts worth about $10). After receiving them, if I don't wish to receive any more books, I can return the shipping statement marked "cancel." If I don't cancel, I will receive 4 brand-new novels every month and be billed just $4.30 per book in the U.S. or $4.99 per book in Canada. That's a savings of at least 13% off the cover price! It's quite a bargain! Shipping and handling is just 50¢ per book in the U.S. and 75¢ per book in Canada.* I understand that accepting the 2 free books and gifts places me under no obligation to buy anything. I can always return a shipment and cancel at any time. Even if I never buy another book, the two free books and gifts are mine to keep forever.

145/345 HDN FVXQ

Name _____ (PLEASE PRINT) _____

Address _____ Apt. # _____

City _____ State/Prov. _____ Zip/Postal Code _____

Signature (if under 18, a parent or guardian must sign)

Mail to the Harlequin® Reader Service:
IN U.S.A.: P.O. Box 1867, Buffalo, NY 14240-1867
IN CANADA: P.O. Box 609, Fort Erie, Ontario L2A 5X3

Want to try two free books from another line?
Call 1-800-873-8635 or visit www.ReaderService.com.

* Terms and prices subject to change without notice. Prices do not include applicable taxes. Sales tax applicable in N.Y. Canadian residents will be charged applicable taxes. Offer not valid in Quebec. This offer is limited to one order per household. Not valid for current subscribers to Harlequin Kiss books. All orders subject to credit approval. Credit or debit balances in a customer's account(s) may be offset by any other outstanding balance owed by or to the customer. Please allow 4 to 6 weeks for delivery. Offer available while quantities last.

Your Privacy—The Harlequin® Reader Service is committed to protecting your privacy. Our Privacy Policy is available online at www.ReaderService.com or upon request from the Harlequin Reader Service.

We make a portion of our mailing list available to reputable third parties that offer products we believe may interest you. If you prefer that we not exchange your name with third parties, or if you wish to clarify or modify your communication preferences, please visit us at www.ReaderService.com/consumerschoice or write to us at Harlequin Reader Service Preference Service, P.O. Box 9062, Buffalo, NY 14269. Include your complete name and address.

HKI3

SPECIAL EXCERPT FROM

 HARLEQUIN

KISS™

Louisa George brings you her debut story

BACKSTAGE WITH HER EX

Nate shoved his hands in his pockets and inhaled, inadvertently breathing in the smell of… Yeah, sunshine. Stupid as it sounded. Like a lame lyric destined for the trash, but it was true—there was something fresh and new and bright about her.

"Sure, we've been working on a few of your hits already. They love your stuff." Her nose wrinkled as she gave him a brief smile. "Maybe you could stay for a little while after and do some autographs…at least for the choir members."

"I'm not planning on hanging round and having a big happy reunion with anyone. I don't see the point in nostalgia, do you?"

She blinked, a slight catch in her throat as she spoke. "No. No, not at all. The past is best left alone. Agreed?"

"Couldn't have said it better myself." Repetition made reality. *The past is best left alone.* Including ex-girlfriends who had started to haunt his dreams.

In truth he should have got Dario to sort this, like usual, Nate was far too busy to deal with schedules. So call it self-indulgent or just plain dumb, but the thought of seeing her before he went back to L.A. appealed. More than he wanted to admit.

She was his connection to his past, the experiences that had shaped him, given him the verve to fight hard for what he wanted.

A vibe hovered between them. He'd had lots of vibes before with lots of women. But this was bigger, stronger than ever. He ignored it. Tried to ignore it.

But he couldn't help looking at her, mesmerized by how the simple halter-neck dress with the daisy pattern and flared skirt, the same blue as her eyes, accentuated her fine collarbones. How her hair looked pull-down ready, and how his hand itched to reach out and let the curls flow over her shoulders.

She was gorgeous. Not Cara gorgeous, but then he'd spent a lot of time trying to work out which parts of her were real and which were fake. Certainly, her outspoken ministrations of everlasting love had been false. Everlasting. Pah. In Hollywood *everlasting* meant five minutes. But then, Sasha had promised him a lifetime, too, and look where that had ended.

Man, this was wild. He forced out a breath. He'd forgotten all about her, consigned her to bad history and pushed her to the dark recesses of his brain. Now here she was, invading every thought, his space, the flame of her red hair looking pretty darned perfect against the cream couch.

Self-indulgence had been too costly in the past and he'd do well to remember that. Sasha might have held his heart once, but she'd damned near thrashed it, too. Taking her to bed would be mighty fine, but he'd never trust her with anything more. Never again.

**Pick up BACKSTAGE WITH HER EX
by Louisa George, on sale September 17,
wherever Harlequin® books are sold.**

Surviving the bridesmaid blues!

AVAILABLE SEPTEMBER 17!

LAST GROOM STANDING
by *USA TODAY* Bestselling Author Kimberly Lang

Dylan Brookes wears a wedding tux better than anyone, but all Marnie wants to do is get beneath it! Sensible Dylan's not ready to give up his bachelor status quite yet, but can Marnie prove to him that sometimes taking a risk is worth it?